CW01432059

Pretty Ugly

KIRSTY GUNN

Pretty Ugly

Landfall
TAURAKA
OTAGO UNIVERSITY PRESS
Te Whare Tā o Ōtākou Whakaihu Waka

Pretty Ugly is the inaugural title in the **Landfall Tauraka** series of short story collections.
Series editor: Chris Prentice

The author wishes to acknowledge the encouragement and support she received from the late Vincent O'Sullivan in the publication of these stories. He was a great friend, a great writer and is greatly missed.

'This ugly of mine, Reader, is to do with considering how much a person's life can bear ...'

Extract from a book reading given for *Pretty Ugly*

Contents

Blood Knowledge

There was something wrong with the garden. You couldn't see it, nothing was obvious. There were no strange plants organised in certain shapes or sinister-looking growths and weeds; the paths were orderly, and the lawns. Roses grew, and pinks, in the places that had been set out for them, and in autumn, berries came out on the crab apple trees along the west side of the wall beside the vegetable plot. It was lovely, actually.

Even so, something was not right. And never had been. Venetia—'the beautiful Venice' her husband Richard called her—might have pointed, with a long white finger, to the stunted pines that clung together by the gate and boundary. Those stiff black branches that would wave wildly in a storm, she could have used them by way of example. But they were nothing out of the ordinary either. Douglas firs were good for a garden, Richard said; they massed and gave protection. Half the reason they could grow the things they did, he told her, was because of those strong trees that you could see from her study window. 'Like sentinels,' is how Richard described them. He loved it, the garden. 'It is everything to me,' he joked. 'More than the house, even.'

'Not more than me, though, surely?' Venetia, 'the beautiful Venice', his city of palazzos and canals, would say to him, in turn.

And, 'silly', would be his unchanging reply.

So forget about a place of odd or frightening plants with thorns or savage leaves and stalks, Richard had made it a haven, the three-quarters of an acre that surrounded their home, and a haven it had been when they'd first moved here, all those years ago before the children were born. He used the word 'haven' then. Because after the stresses of his City job, there it was. A safe place for the two of them with everything growing and flourishing as it should.

And they still talked about it that way, didn't they? That the garden, like everything, everything in their life, would be as they would want it? It was a conversation between the two of them that had factored a sort of faith in the decisions that they had made together. A belief. Only the reality was, Venetia knew, that the wife who each day applied fresh makeup to her face, drawing on, before the mirror, a fine dark pink or crimson lipstick mouth, also knew the very earth from which the garden was made held something secretive and so peculiar that it could spoil everything. And that it was there, that knowledge, and that the garden had the capacity to keep it, no matter what she and Richard said, long after their deaths. Forever actually. It was bedded in.

She never spoke about any of this out loud, of course. Instead, she went out in the mornings with her cup of coffee, her favourite cup, the one with the golden rim, and looked across the lawns, admiring the hedge by the gate with its uniform shape, the fuchsia and honeysuckle that had been planted to look wild in the far corner. It had been such a long time now since they'd moved here and fashioned the garden to be the way it was, so why not—irrespective of her feelings—admire it? After all, nothing had changed. The family had all been well, there'd been no concerns or disappointments. She and Richard were in good health, and he'd made so much money in that job of his they couldn't help but feel contented; the four children grown up with families and careers of their own by now but coming home all the time for lovely holidays and visits. There was Emma, who they'd always called Baby, with a baby of her own now, living in the next village, and Tom and Susannah and Evan busy in London as ever … It's true, Venetia, the lovely Venetia thought, as she arranged one of her pale blue or rose or emerald-coloured shawls around her shoulders before sitting down to her desk every day to work, that she'd had nothing, nothing to trouble her through this long period of marriage and family, of domestic life. In fact, you might say—and she did, she reminded herself of this often, and more now she was older, putting on her lipstick in the morning, checking, before the mirror, that the colour was right—she'd had everything for herself that she might have expected. You could use this phrase if you like: A perfect life.

In fact, 'silly', Richard would say again, if she was to bring up the subject of doing things differently, as she used to do sometimes in the early years, talking then about moving away, maybe, or going to live abroad for a time—as though they might take a break from what they were building up around them or even escape it altogether. For 'silly' it must have been to think that he would leave the position he'd attained in the firm, one of the most prestigious in London, or that she herself would give up the writing commissions that by then were already creating a lifestyle for her, of working to contract, one novel every couple of years like clockwork, like a machine. Even so, she would talk sometimes, back then when the children were young and later, too, about how they might live somewhere else. 'Be different,' as she used to describe it, as though she knew about it already as 'that other life'.

'But why would you have such a silly idea?' was always Richard's response. 'Be somewhere different? As though we were different people? When we have everything as we need it here? Everything.'

'Because ...' she might begin, his 'beautiful Venice,' each of her lovely shawls a gift from him and a new colour chosen for every passing year. 'Because ...?'

And 'shhh' he would reply, drawing her to him, taking in his hands her long white fingers, caressing her rings and gems. 'My city of palazzos and canals ...' he would murmur. 'Shhh, now. Silly.'

For this reason, Richard's sweet 'shhhh', his love of quietness, and the daily routine of life, the various requirements of work and domesticity that increased over time, it had been many years since she'd talked about where they lived, suggesting that they might find another way of feeling at home. And it was hardly the time now, with Richard about to retire for good in a year's time, to start bringing up those sorts of thoughts again, finding ways of introducing them into a conversation. So why was she doing that? Just recently? Interrupting herself, and him? Why imagine at this late point in their lives, change? For it was measured out, surely it was, their remaining future, fixed, with Richard already planning certain activities in advance of all the extra time he would soon have to spend. A greenhouse, that was the next idea, built in the Edwardian style and great for parties, he said. 'Lots and lots of parties.' And that they'd be able to sit out there as well, just the two of them, even in the winter months if they wanted to, among, oh, what? Orange trees and tropical flowers? Anything. He had already spoken to architects and was laying out a ground. 'Look darling ...' Three weeks ago he'd started digging in the back lawn. They'd be able to see from the large imagined glassed-in room, he said, all the tiny geraniums he'd grown from seed, pale pink and lemon and soft, baby blue they were pictured on the packet and that he'd been tending on the windowsill of his potting shed through the winter and early spring, promising her, that phrase she hated, 'a show, a real show.'

Dear Richard, despite his awful job. Digging away. Preparing for something he called a 'show'. How he knew nothing about it. Fiddling with his little seeds. In so many ways he was like a young boy, a child, as though he'd never been the kind of lawyer he'd turned into, while all the time, throughout their marriage, she'd been fully grown. And here they were now, Venetia supposed, the pair of them, old. With a massive payout on the way, pensions, benefits … Yes, old. Though hard to believe, she found herself saying to friends, speaking in the kinds of clichés that people expected, using that easy vocabulary of a certain kind of life. 'Hard to believe,' when the years had 'rushed by' so quickly, one book after another … And there was nothing much to worry about there either, never had been. From the first title, all that time ago when they were just married, she'd been writing the series that her publishers adored, a 'global trend', is how they described it. It had just gone on and on.

'No need to stop now, sweetheart,' her editor had joked with her on his last call. 'The Japanese translation is about to come out over there, and that's the beginning of a whole new market for you if you want it.'

'Want it?' she'd replied and laughed. She had an airy, tinkling laugh her friends loved. 'I don't seem to have much choice.' She was looking down at her hands splayed on the fine walnut surface of her desk, her editor on the speakerphone saying something about 'marketing budgets'. Her hands were so white, even after all these years; she'd looked after them. 'What sells is what's wanted,' she said. 'I know that by now.' She flexed her long fingers, admiring them still, and all her rings. 'But don't worry,' she'd finished. 'I've already had some ideas that would work well in the Far East. I've started on something, in fact.'

'Good for you,' Richard said, as he did every time she told him about another sale, a new contract. It was the way her life was.

A story here, then the next, and the next ... Everything in order and 'one novel every two years, like clockwork', remember? Hadn't she written that down somewhere? 'No need to stop now' like a refrain, like a machine? 'Beautiful Venice.' 'My city of palazzos and canals ...' When she stood in front of the mirror sometimes, after applying her lipstick in the morning or when removing makeup at night, she might open her mouth so wide she could see right inside herself into her own dark workings. That was who she really was.

And the garden would keep its secret. The children had grown up enclosed by its walls and flowers—what were they to imagine anything different? That a place may have another, shrunken life within? A sort of shadow, was it? Another self? For that's how it felt to her, stepping in the gate, whenever she'd been away, whatever time of day or night, or season, back then, or now ... The feeling that she'd returned to somewhere else that was a separate story, a place with its plots, its hidden corners, that was also home. 'My beautiful Venice.' She might think about the garden's story but need never say.

People don't speak of half the things they could, of course, or want to—she used to tell herself that was the case with the book writing, too. That you just get it down, write what you can. Let the narrative play out in the way readers want it to: a piece of information here, another detail there. Historical romance gave you all kinds of rules to follow, which is what made it easy to write—is what she'd thought from the beginning and told the magazines when they came to interview her, said the same on radio and TV. Her first *Home is Where* ... had been an instant success. 'You're onto something,' her publishers had said from the beginning, historical stories with domestic themes were 'global, marketable. What's not to like?' And Richard always encouraging her, of course. 'Your editors have the right idea. Keep the books coming, darling.' He loved the series, the beautiful predictability of it, the stately arrival of each new title and all that came with it. 'Ah, my city of palazzos and canals,' he toasted her, with every publication. 'My shining star.' And the children, too, 'It's true, you're brilliant, Mum,' they joined in. 'My friends even say their parents read your books!'

'And now we'll be able to build the studio off the back of the garage.'

'And get a classic car. And the flat in London?'

'You're famous, kind of.'

'You should never stop.'

'Yet I come in the garden gate ...' she could hear the words articulate in her mind as clearly as when she'd heard them all those years ago, whispering in the trees. 'And I know ...' she could hear, as though reading the words now, as though they were clustered together on a page before her, 'because I've proven it to myself. That it's not right here. Not right, where I live.'

Of course, no one would believe her; they would laugh out loud if she were to come close to expressing any of this. Not that she ever would. She had never spoken much about herself; motherhood made that aspect of things easy. Children don't want to learn, why should they, who their parents really are. And she and Richard would have no need to talk about themselves, what a bore that would be. They had a great marriage. Really, there was nothing to worry about. They wanted for nothing. She was fanciful, that's all. Friends said it, everyone. 'You make things up, it's why you're a writer'—though doing the romantic histories was not at all like real writing, she knew. The *Home is Where* ... series wrote itself. It was a case of doing the research, compiling the characters, and the contents would play out in the same way with every title: Tough times into good. Happy ever after. Wars could rage in Renaissance England, French coasts beset by nineteenth-century piracy and Highland estates overcome by rebellion … but all would come right in the end because it was what happened at home that counted; it was a story after all. Fanciful? 'What is fanciful,' the garden always said back to her, when she looked out of the window of her study some days while working on this chapter or that, editing the final section where everything becomes resolved and history settles into the one we know from books, 'what is real and remembered and made out of truth and lies, is what I present you with here. My black branches and my twisted vines that won't stop growing. My rich soil. The fancy you're accused of, woman,' the garden said, 'is in me.'

So. 'My beautiful Venice'. This is where she was. In the midst of this life with its parade of family and friends taking their turns before her, sitting down at her walnut desk in the mornings, managing everything meticulously as always, with one new sentence written down, followed by the next, each new paragraph arriving on the page in orderly procession to make up the kind of fiction everyone wanted to read, only living on the surface of things, as though there was nothing dug in, no darkness inside. Was how she'd lived her calendared life. Month by month, season into season, year into year, walking through her days with her face made up for each one of them, dressed in the shawls that were her gifts, quartz and rose and silver, emerald coloured, her long fingers bright with gems and rings. And that there was something 'wrong' with the garden … Why write that down, even? Why be thinking about bringing up to the light now the tiny pieces of paper covered in her own miniature handwriting that she'd kept closed away in boxes and files for all these years? Why be getting them out, those tickets and bill stubs and receipts that were also maps and codes and records of the most private excitements? To be wanting to display in the wide air those scraps and bits and make something of them, another kind of history and nothing like the sort she normally produced that was hidden away in the garden in places that only she and the garden knew? 'Imagine.' She said the word out loud, though none of this was imagined, it was real. Because she was doing that. Getting out, from where they'd been hidden, the pieces of thin paper she'd written on all those years ago, and … 'Imagine,' she said it again. If she was to arrange them now, those same papers, in sequence, and expose them. That dark mouth of hers, wide open in the mirror, letting out the secrets, telling another kind of story that had already been laid down.

For she was 'My city of palazzos and canals.' And surely so it must remain? In fact, write that out exactly: 'Surely so it must remain, that the story that has been written of success and beauty and marriage and wealth must be the story that should remain.' Because it was a familiar and loved story. All of it engaging and planned and jingling with bracelets and gems. 'Our fortune for the fortunate,' as the children used to say. Yet here she was now, letting this other in. 'There was something wrong with the garden …' She'd started it already.

And there was Richard … in the same garden digging and planting and rooting out weeds, composting from waste. Slipping fresh cuttings into the soil and they would be nurtured and allowed to grow … Richard. Richard. Richard. As far as he was concerned, there was nothing to worry about, no not at all. As far as he was concerned it was only going on, their life together, as it always had. As he dug and mowed, tied back and pruned. Out there in all seasons. He'd planted daffodils around the tree stumps down where the cherry trees were and they came up, a mass of yellow every spring and more of them each time, another 'show'. Speaking to her this way with his hands in the soil. As she watched him. 'A lovely show.'

He would not say anything different because of course he didn't know what kind of soil he was digging, or about anything, not the real knowledge, deep down. He would want everything to flourish, Richard would. That it would all grow. Lawyers were straightforward that way. They saw things in black and white, words on a page that were nothing like the words of this story that was coming together here, oh, yes. Who knew where it could go? Of course she still had the current *Home is Where* … to finish and notes for the next one made, with people contacting her from all over the world as they always did to tell her how much they loved them. 'We love the series!' 'We love the books!' 'Please write some more!' So she would naturally seem to carry on with that, with the routine of her work, as she had always done, through all the years of sharing her life with her husband, the children growing up in the house around her, the *Home is Where* … years. The Home is … here, there, wherever it is years. Going on and on and on.

'I simply can't wait for the next *Home is Where* …' a woman from New York had written to her just last week to say. 'Whatever the period or setting, I know I'm going to love it. I've read them all.' She 'could hardly stop now,' could she?

But one morning, she looked at herself in the mirror and knew she could. She set down the lipstick she'd just finished applying, and instead of arranging around her shoulders the soft white shawl she had chosen to wear that day she brought it up to her mouth like a great cloth and used it to wipe the cosmetic off her lips. A dark streak of red ran down the length of the expensive fabric. The thing was ruined. She bundled it up and put it straight in the bin, her heart racing. It was as though she'd come to life again after a long time of being asleep.

The children had said for a while that she might want to write for herself—a break from the contract work she'd been tied to for all the years. They'd encouraged it even, giving her pretty notebooks and sets of Moleskines for Christmas; Evan once brought home a big stack of yellow legal pads for 'your life project' as he called it. The new activity she'd started had nothing to do with being that sort of a mother, though. The phrases and lines being scribbled in secret on scraps of paper and on the back of bills only reminded her of the hidden writing from all those years ago, the same nameless words coming out into the open and being got down frantically, breathlessly, between other tasks and they frightened her, as they'd frightened her before, though she was exhilarated, too, quietly, privately, by what she discovered she had done. When she found herself in her study going through a bin for a bit of gift wrap that was crumpled and torn, and smoothing it out, and writing quickly, frenziedly even, an awful little group of words on the back of that, before a family lunch one day in early spring ... Then she knew things had become turned for her indeed.

So she fell behind, deliberately, with the *Home is Where ...* They asked about it, her publishers, then the family, but she was vague in her answers. At first, she said she was still working on it, then that she'd had an extension, that the contract had been redrafted, that was it, and anyhow, yes, she was a bit bored, but of course she would get onto it and the book would be finished in time for the autumn launches as usual.

'Dad will be retiring next year,' one of the boys, Tom, said, helping her in the kitchen. It had been his birthday; the paper she'd written that last strange piece on had been a leftover from the brightly coloured gift wrap she'd used for his new jersey. 'So why not just give up the series if you want to?' He'd been helping her tidy up after the party, after they'd finished celebrating, sung Happy Birthday, eaten most of the cake. 'Both of you can start taking it easy, spend more time in the garden or whatever. Dad told me he wants to build you a conservatory ...'

She'd moved away from him, she remembers now, so he couldn't see her face.

'Mum?'

An image of that part of the lawn, where Richard had told her the new building was to be, rising up at her, not grass at all but graves …

'Mum, I was talking to you. Is everything alright?'

Was where she was so far. She stopped wearing the shawls, her brace-lets, the rings. Her hands were white, but they were unadorned, and by now she could see quite clearly how old they were. She laid them down before her again on the fine walnut surface of her desk and splayed her fingers. What do you do, she thought, here in her study, or when she woke in the night or stepped in the front gate with it all there before her? What do you do if the life you are living right now, that always seemed to be enough … what do you do if you know, as the garden knew, that there was more? On the piece of paper, the wrapping paper from the bin, she'd written the word 'garden' three times, underlining it, and then arranging the words backwards, around and about as though an anagram, finding other words in the letters that she could use: 'den' yes, and 'rag', and then also 'red'. She circled each one and then folded the paper into a tiny square no larger than a postage stamp. It was something she knew she would be able to use.

Back in the beginning, when she'd first married, she'd spent a lot of time in the garden. She'd helped Richard then, on the weekends when he started going out there as much as he could, and during the week as well, in the summer, as a break from work, how he'd needed it. Together they'd planted that forsythia by the back wall, making a kitchen garden beside the path leading to it, walling it in and building raised beds. She herself had designed and planted the rose circle in the middle of the front lawn—an idea she'd had since she was a little girl, she told Richard, out of a book of fairy tales. These activities, a narrative of sorts running along beside the other, were when she was expecting Susannah, her firstborn child, that one carried to term and then safely delivered; three more following over the next five years in neat succession. It had been busy, that period of her life, with the babies and the work involved in looking after them; she'd been almost stilled into submission by how much there was to do … until she reverted again to the other habit. A set of telephone bills, cut up into strips and covered in her beautifully inked and finished microscopic writing that was not easy to decipher reminded her of that time. For she had tried, she had. But she'd researched so much for her books about gardens and herbs and flowers and what women could do with them that it had been almost too easy, from the outset, to turn her work with Richard into another kind of planting. He had always loved that she had ideas for the various beds and variations of seed and would never know about the amount of stuff she had in there, among the geraniums and clouds of baby's breath, that could poison.

This was all being written down now, and on different papers and bits, the order of it, the sequence, of what she'd done. How early it had started. How long. How, despite trying to stop it, when life had seemed to get better and better, the other thing had never ceased happening. Not before the children, when she was newly married, and not after. She kept doing it, over and over. She worked out once it may have been as many as nine times. The cramping and the morning sickness, that feeling, and being dizzy and nauseous, having to lie down suddenly, in the middle of the day, or finding herself vomiting what looked like black bile … Sometimes it felt continuous. She'd made it seem as though she was taking care of herself in the way people said you should at that time of your life. 'A special, special time in the life of a woman,' they all said, '—to get plenty of rest, eat properly, to take a bit of gentle exercise …' But she'd been able to twist it, change it, without anyone knowing, and the feeling of attainment each time—as she'd recorded, so carefully, in writing so small—was absolute.

The first time it happened, realising she could do this—could force— obtain an outcome that would be different to what nature intended and have it effected by her own hand, was when they'd been in the house for just six months, newly married and everything going so well; she'd just signed the contract for the first two-book deal. Life had seemed secure. Richard was on track to be made partner, and though working all hours, the money was going to be out of this world, an amazing opportunity for him, he said. He would never be able to walk away. She remembered him in those early years, how he would come home at night to her, how they had been together. He'd talked about having a family from the moment they'd first met, about being parents with lots of children and a busy, happy home. These were words and phrases he'd been using with her since she'd met him. Being a mother, a father someday—isn't that what most people wanted, what we were here for, after all? 'Who knows?' he would say, as he headed out the door to work the next morning. 'Any minute now darling, you're going to tell me you're pregnant.'

Venetia wrote that down, as a complete sentence, 'Any minute now, darling …' then put a line through it and hid it away with a doll's-size stack of new papers in the back of the drawer of her desk, along with her old notes and receipts.

'I suppose …' she'd answered him, all those years ago, her face turned away or her back to him as she worked … while the garden was there outside the window, looking in on her, coming in at the windows of the house, forcing itself, that low dark branch. 'I suppose …' and 'Of course …' and 'I agree …' she'd said. All of it coming together by now as though it was happening again as she read it, written in her own way, in her own way and full of her own rich content, every bit as much a narrative as any of the other fiction she used to write, and more—exposed in tiny words on a small piece of paper clipped to others with a pin that the first time, using their own flowers and herbs, it was actually breathtakingly easy. She had not told Richard she thought she was pregnant, not knowing why, when she knew how much he wanted it, but the minute she confirmed it for herself had gone immediately to the health food shop in the village and bought the only other part of the recipe she needed, aware exactly of how much to use and what to do. 'All my historical research …' she had written down on the back of a shopping list she'd kept from that time. It had worked, instantly, easily. She miscarried after just one week, and it was as nothing to bury the dirtied towel out by the back wall. On a torn-off corner of an envelope she'd drawn a tiny map and stitched a cross to mark the spot. 'Here,' it said. How she loved seeing it again. The next time, too, was straightforward—though the one after that, not long after, took more time. She'd been worried when nothing happened that she must have built up some kind of immunity to the herbs she'd been using, or women would have used them all the time, wouldn't they? Back in those hardened days of endless pregnancies and life-threatening manual labour? She waited one week, as before, then two, five … Finally it was in the sixth week when the discharge came and she couldn't stop vomiting endlessly, shamelessly. Richard kept asking if it might be morning sickness and she could only shake her head. The minute he was out the door to work, she gathered up the mess she'd hidden in the laundry basket and found another secret place to bury it, away from the others, over in the corner of the lawn where it was already being turned over for a new rose bed and the earth was soft and warm when she laid the pieces of her work into it. 'Finished,' she read now, written on the back of a cinema ticket, where she had drawn another tiny map and made a mark. When she looked down again at those hands of hers, she could see how it was as though they were drenched in dirt.

After that, she didn't buy the fixatives and other herbs she needed in the village; she could no longer justify that amount of research. So she drove to London and purchased a whole trolley full of things she didn't need by way of disguising the amount of little brown bottles and extracts, concentrates, she'd bought in one go. The girl ringing them up at the till had given her a look, 'You know what this is for, right?' she'd said. 'Just be careful—you probably know—if you're ever wanting to get pregnant. It's not great, this stuff, for that.' It had been like a short story, Venetia had thought, the visit, the shop … Though not quite. For the way she'd written about it, the sensation of being in the shop, at large in the wide supermarket-like aisles of the place, buying these things, knowing what they could do, the sense of achievement … That wasn't something anyone would want to read. Nor how, with the bought ingredients, easily, efficiently, twice more, and with the same combinations but in greater quantities, she'd been able to get the same result. She knew about certain exercises, things you could do, so when the usual doses didn't seem to fix on the sixth pregnancy, she used a kind of prod she'd made herself in the bath one night when Richard was out at a Christmas do for work. Its effect was immediate and terrible to see, all through the warm water, and she'd had to get up straight away to put on her outdoor things to go out into the garden and find a place where she could dig before he came home.

That time, she thought she might have stopped with it, in herself. The thing she'd used had given her an infection. It had taken the best part of an hour to break the frozen ground and make a trough that was deep enough, and she'd been cold right through to the bone.

She'd thought at first it was flu, but no, a full-on blood infection was what she ended up with and she'd had to go to hospital where she had wild dreams about walking all four corners of the garden where the results of what she had done were buried and all the pieces of paper she'd used to write about it were fluttering about and she couldn't gather them up. She woke wide-eyed in the middle of the night to a nurse in the room with her, an older woman, and wept with relief. And it was for that reason, some kind of crisis, perhaps? Caused by being so ill? Seeing the love and concern on her husband's face the next day? Something. But the following pregnancy she let sit inside her and carried to term, and the next and the next and the next. 'Four lovely babies in the house,' was the phrase she used.

And 'Look at you,' Richard said. 'My city of palazzos and canals. You're magnificent.'

And yes, you'd think, she would have thought—that would be the end of it. But three years after Emma's birth she realised she was pregnant again, and that was the beginning of the cycle starting up as though she had never had a child and given birth and nursed and cared for it. Miscarriage wasn't the right word, she thought, for what she was doing to herself—though she'd kept using that word for it. 'Miscarriage'. It was written and scored through, over and over, in her wad of pinned writings that she'd kept from that time. *Miscarriage*, she wrote down again now. But the word … No. That was for something carried wrongly. Mis-Carriage. For something meant to be safely held that hadn't been. What she'd effected weren't miscarriages, nor were they abortions, or procedures of any kind. They were … *Conclusions.* Is how she now realised she had always thought of these performances of hers. Conclusions. Completions. She wrote it down. A conclusion, that sense of having achieved exactly what she had planned. Conclusions, again and again, as the doses became higher and the things she did to herself more extreme. The herbs for the final three were deathly strong; there had been some kind of metal extract involved in the mixture and she felt for months afterwards in all three cases the enormity of what she had done, but then it was over. She would never carry a child inside her again.

After that last time Richard had been concerned, she'd detected, perhaps thinking that the change of life might bring about something in her, some factor he hadn't counted on, that he might have to be careful about, take precautions. It was just like before, all those years ago, after her having to stay in hospital, when he had feared there might be no children after all. He had hidden his disappointment then, as he hid his fears later, potting out geraniums in the tool shed, putting in tomato plants and gooseberry bushes and raspberry canes—all these things engineered for their fruiting. 'My beautiful Venice' had felt herself to be stronger, after that time in hospital—she'd written it down as another kind of ugly, broken short story, on the back of a menu card, how she'd told the same nurse who used to come in to her room to sit and watch over her, everything, everything, and vowed never to do what she'd done to herself again. But then, of course, she had. Even through the births of four children that had followed that episode, the quiet certainty that she would had lurked, darkened, and now that she'd brought all the pieces together, all the scraps and tiny bound papers, the stitched and stapled fragments into a narrative of sorts, she saw completely how the process she'd been engaged with, her own 'life project', would have always had its way with her to the end. She'd written it down, even. 'The secrets she had kept,' she read, in a beautiful ink, 'also secrets she would want to hold.'

Finally, it was this knowledge, more than anything else, her family, her marriage, her career, that gave her the sense of herself she realises now she'd always needed. A sense of private achievement, another history permeating the one she had made for herself with a husband and family and career and staining it with her own colours, lending to it her own powerful essence. Even now, when she was old, she saw other mothers with their babies in the street, the special smiles those women reserved for their infants, their attention to their little bodies—and she felt triumphant. That she'd both known—had had and had also not had—that same experience. It had been exactly as she'd wanted after all.

'Seriously, darling,' Richard had said when she'd last suggested to him—before she'd started writing this and putting all the bits of paper together for this other kind of story she'd never thought she would write, let alone finish—that maybe it was not too late. That they could recover something of the part of themselves they'd lost in choosing the lives they had, doing what they had done and all of it, really, yes all of it, only for themselves, themselves, themselves. 'What on earth are you going on about? What on earth do you mean?' He'd seemed so worried, she remembered, putting it down now on the page, his face all at once shadowed, and so grave and sad, that she'd had to quickly pretend it was nothing, that she'd just been reading something in a magazine and it had made her go off on a tangent, that's all, having a bit of fun. Of course, she should have known better, that from the very beginning of their lives together it had already been too late for any of that. She took his hand, she remembered, by now so behind with the other deadline that she wondered if she would ever be able to get back to it, start all that all over again. *Home is Where* … Where was it again? Here. There. Nowhere.

So, 'conclusion' then. It was the right word. Conclusion, conclusion, conclusion … There from the start and the description exactly for where she'd wanted this story to go. Over and over, conclusion—as if the mere writing of it again might bring her to some kind of final remark about the choices she'd made, this private, private life she'd willed to open up inside her and patch through as a kind of excrement into the grounds of the very place where she lived. Conclusion. All conclusion. She'd wanted, in her own words, from the beginning, to bring it about. Just as she had said her own name out loud into the air with every burying, as though it were an announcement, a mighty enactment: My name is Venetia Elizabeth Margaret Alton. This is my work. This is who I am.

And Richard was an old man by now, is how he looked to her; she'd be old herself to anyone looking on at all this. A life contracted, forged. There could be no other. Because the world she'd made for herself, the world she'd always talked of finding, that 'different life', that other world, well, it was right here around them, in the soil, under their feet. It was written down, from start to finish. In scraps and pieces, maybe, but all concluded and threaded together and connected … In the end, you might say, also the beginning. Because 'There was something wrong with the garden,' remember? She'd started that way. Every single thing done to herself, by herself, created and finished and then created and finished again … The feeling she ends with, as glorious to her now as it ever was, of putting a blanket out under the trees in the orchard in summertime, the four children tumbling upon it like puppies, while knowing in the ground around her was all that blood.

❦

Blackjack

By the time she got up to her room she'd decided she wasn't going to stay. First thing in the morning it would have to be, because it was too late to leave now. She would have missed the last flight back down, and facing that long train ride again ... was out of the question. So it would have to be tomorrow. But first thing. Because she couldn't stay here. She couldn't.

Checking in, she'd wondered for the umpteenth time what she was doing even being in this situation in the first place—thinking about it all day on the train for that matter. Letting the kids talk her into it, a date with a stranger, staying overnight and all the rest of it. What kind of a madcap idea was that, at her age? Brendan had said everyone does it, Mum, and had set the whole thing up with Kit agreeing. That their father had been gone for a year now and she was still young, that it was time she met someone new, they said, and that they would just go ahead and register her on an app they'd seemed very excited about, scrolling through images at a pitch and downing their gin and tonics. Then it was a case of ... This one? That one? What about him? And he looks nice, doesn't he, Kit had said, peering into the image on the screen as if she could read the man's heart right there. He's a bit like Dad, even, don't you think? And look, Mum, he likes the things you do. See? The symphony, and all that? They've got a great performing arts centre up there. And you can't stay in the house forever, miles from everyone. It will do you good.

So, alright then, she had let them organise. She would 'meet' him, whoever he was, after she'd booked into the hotel he'd suggested where they could have a leisurely breakfast the next day and then wander round the city, if they got on, taking it in. He was from a small town, too, the kids said. He'd also lost his wife about a year ago and was learning to get over it.

But what did that really mean, 'get over it'? You don't get over a thing like that. Jonny gone … the feeling of it was enormous. And Brendan and Kit? Well, they had no idea. Of the relief. The comfort of it. The new vast calm. The house was like a church now that their father was actually out of it, away for good and never coming back. So why would she have wanted to leave that peace and quiet to be here, in this awful place? It had been built for gambling. As soon as she walked through the enormous glass doors leading into the lobby, she could see that. People were dealing at tables right there by where she'd had to register. Hearts, darling. Hearts. Clubs. Aces. Why did everything to do with card games sound so mean? It was because they were mean, that's why. Bridge. Poker. Gin Rummy. All the ghastly combinations and the chances and losses of them … along with the people who played … terrifying. Her voice was shaking when she gave her name to the young woman behind the desk who took her time and then handed over the keys. 'Room 1606,' she said. 'Sounds like a lucky number, eh?' By then she felt she could barely breathe.

Because no one had any idea. No one. About all that stuff with Jonny and luck, bloody luck. How it had been, and for years and years. No idea. Oh, the odd card game with neighbours, the occasional family holiday with a visit to the casino, maybe, the fun of the slot machines and the children's cries of delight at the quick heavy rush of coins. But they had not known the half of it. Not close to half. Nor of all that went with it—nearly losing the house that one time, and the drinking and those women their father used to take up with when he was gone off on one his jags … remember them? Knocking on the door at all hours and wanting to come in and wait for him? Or on the phone late at night, screaming down the line when would he be back? It was a wonder she was not the one dead; with the amount of stuff she'd had to keep separate from Brendan and little Katherine when they were young and growing up. A wonder she was not the one sick and cremated and gone forever into ashes with the amount she'd had to keep from herself, for that matter, to learn not to think about it, even.

Yet here she was, thinking about it now. As though gone back into that life—back, back, back—pushed into it by those same children, now adults themselves, and with a view to her meeting some man here they'd found for her online. Was she really so ruined by her long marriage that she hadn't thought in the first place that there'd been something wrong about that app and couldn't have said to them from the beginning: What on Earth are you thinking? But there had been that phrase, 'He looks a bit like Dad'—and her not being able to reply. And that, too, part of her keeping the story of their father bright for them, for the children, despite everything. So she'd found herself walking through the ghastly front door of a trap, is what it was, putting down her overnight bag on its floor, fishing out her credit card. As though he was still with her, the man she'd married. Right there beside her in the lobby, with his: Go on darling, just sign the damn form. Good girl. That's my baby. All—back, back, back.

For how he would have loved it here. Room 1606. All that. Black Jonny. It was his kind of place and his kind of people in it. She could hear them—even up here in the hotel room—as though the low terrible hum of their concentration, their powerful immobility in the grip of what they were doing, was in the very sound of the air conditioner, in the atmosphere held in the space containing the bed and the window and the chair. What kind of man would want to meet in a hotel like this? Symphony orchestras, my eye. Theatre and chamber music. It would have been lies, like it was always lies. It was changing money for chips, is what it was. Spinning the wheel and turning cards into one endless play that finished in being dead. That is all that had ever happened to the kind of man who would want to come here, the kind she'd married. How had she ever managed to keep it, all of it, clear away from her own shining babies? That their father would never show himself to them the way he'd shown himself to her, from after the very first of those trips of his away. Coming home Daddy. But not Daddy. Only a someone else instead with a mean card's name and his black, black hair and his black eyes.

Of course she would leave first thing in the morning. Get the first train. Arrive safely at her lovely house, and there would be the concert programme playing on the radio. The garden. A glass of wine or two on a Friday. That was all she needed. All she had ever needed. And stupid, stupid online dating … She closed her eyes. On the way to the lift up to her room she'd passed a group of older men and women at a particularly large table, all with garishly coloured cocktails and pitchers of drinks set beside them but silent as death while the girl in front dealt their cards. As she'd waited for the wretched lift to arrive, as it seemed to take forever, she'd heard one of them suddenly call out 'Hey' and crazily turned. There'd been a man—oh, handsome enough—and a second or two of him looking over at her, his eyes narrowing as he took her in. *Give me some of that luck of yours* … He'd done it just as Jonny would do it. *Go on … Say it* … Looking straight into her, willing her … *Say my name, my real name* ... Looking, willing. *Do it. Say it. Bring me some of that sweet luck of yours, my darling* ... It was as though she knew him entirely. The lift pinged, the doors slid open, and she'd nearly fallen over getting inside. She could hear voices, female voices, screeching 'You bloody flirt. For chrissake! Just play,' as the heavy steel panels closed. They were all of them drunk and now anything could happen, she'd thought then. Anything. She thought it again when, a minute or two later, the doorbell in her room sounded and she opened the door, and the same man was standing there.

Praxis, or Why Joan Collins is Important

'I want to talk to you about Joan,' Anne said, taking me by the arm and leading me into a corner of the room. This was two weeks ago at a party thrown by a mutual friend to celebrate the publication of her book about historic rose gardens of England. There were roses, of course, everywhere.

'It's important,' she said.

So, past enormous china bowls filled with 'Dancing Ballerina', 'Rambling Jack' and 'Iceberg' Anne led me, the names of each arrangement written carefully on cards balanced next to them, along with dates and details of the gardens where they could be found. 'Whisky Galore'; 'Sunset'; 'Faint Hearted'. She found us a spot behind an elegant high-backed sofa where we could be on our own, a large bouquet of 'Celebration' on a table in front to shield us. These displays, each one different from the last and so carefully annotated, were clearly instructive. You might have even said they had a part to play here. My eye, for example, had been drawn to a blue and white amphora of 'Skip-to-my-Lou', set just to the left of Anne on a side table also crowded with glasses and bottles of champagne. 'First planted at Sissinghurst, 1876, cuttings taken for Blenheim, Highgate and Kew early 20th C.' There was surely something significant, I remarked, about the use of all the proper nouns. Something about a rose never being just a rose.

But Anne was having none of it. 'I've made a time to see her tonight,' she said, referring to the actress Joan Collins about whom she was writing a biography. She drained her glass, inured entirely to the charm of petals and scent. 'It's important that a plan is put before her,' she was saying, 'for the new direction the book is taking. It's complicated to explain …' She let her voice drift off, as though she was uncertain, as though something really was complicated, but there was nothing uncertain or complicated about her. Her eyes were bright and her gaze direct. 'Joan is smart as a whip, but she only stays up for half an hour at a time, and there's loads to convey,' Anne said. 'So I need you to come with me.' She set down her glass next to 'Skip-to-my-Lou' and waited for a response. 'To help me tell her, I mean,' she added. 'Now.'

What? At first I could say nothing. Between the large arrangement to Anne's left and another set at my own right elbow, a modest show of 'Old Glory' positioned next to a large and tall lamp beside the sofa as well as the sofa itself and everything Anne had just put to me by way of an opening conversational gambit … well, the whole set-up was quite crowded. I couldn't take it all in. Go there tonight? To Joan Collins' Mayfair home? To go soon? In fact *now*? Why? 'I don't—' I managed.

But Anne was pressing her suit. 'There've been some changes,' she said, 'to the book, big changes. And I want you to be involved in bringing them about. I don't know in what way yet, or what it all means. But I want you to come in on this …' she paused darkly, 'somehow.'

For the second time that evening I had no response. I seemed altogether unable to proceed.

'Somehow?' was all I could come up with. 'Somehow?' I said again. It had been quite hard for us both to squeeze in. The space behind the sofa was narrow, and the thing itself high-backed and stiffly upholstered, the tables set around it jam-crammed with roses and champagne, glasses and bottles full and empty. Then there was the matter of the enormous lamp, stage-lighting the entire effect. Altogether I was feeling constrained. On show. On the spot, even. It was clear I had been given, by Anne, some sort of role. An involvement that she had designed, some conversation already determined that was to take place in the service of implementing upon the manuscript she had in hand these 'big changes' so mentioned. And to learn that my part had been so allocated here? In this corner? At Marjorie's party about roses and her book? To be talking instead about another book, the book Anne was writing about Joan Collins, and about some already organised visit to the actress' Mayfair home? How was I to feel? Off the back of our being surrounded by the heady blooms of 'Whisky' and 'Celebration' and all the rest of it? What was I to do? Didn't I need to do something?

Of course none of this, my sense of uncertainty and uncertainty's sister, imperative, seemed to affect Anne in the slightest. She was already telling me in great detail about where she was with her research and about how the meeting she had lined up for us both with the subject of the biography she'd been working on for some time—spending months in libraries and film archives, interviewing friends and associates and all who could be contacted to speak about 'the starlet turned actress' as Anne kept saying—was pivotal. We needed to go to Joan Collins' house 'now' she said, that very evening, if the book was to be 'the book it needs to be'. The project had undergone a 'seismic shift', she went on, in purpose and construction, somehow all related to that same phrase, 'starlet turned actress' and Joan would need to know, Anne went on to explain, 'about the mighty overturn of paradigm that occurs when one disrupts the concept of "personality" and replaces it instead with the idea of "player"'.

Whew! Pivotal, alright. This happened two weeks ago and my own life has changed, it has, as a result of that particular discussion. Joan Collins' biography has had that effect—a piece of work that might have been straightforward yet was become, through the force of Anne's formidable intellect and robust education in postmodern literary theory, a very different sort of publication. For I think of things differently now, I do, all life seen through the experience of that same 'seismic shift'. I might want to describe Marjorie's party in more definite terms, say, than those that I find I have used here; I think about how I might parse and reimagine the role all of us played, not just by Anne and me but everyone in that room. Certainly I would ask, in any future piece of writing I might undertake: Who were we, really? Those people I've positioned among the roses? I would include in any text this question: What did our actions show? But back then, behind the sofa, I was still onlooker, you might say, spectator to Anne's game. I was a person engaged but not directly involved in the story she was telling me about why Joan Collins was important and so necessary, how her actress life showed all of us the parts we ourselves might come to perform by heart.

'Listen,' I was able to get a word in at last. There'd been much talk by then of Joan's immaculate 'mask', her use of wigs, props, costumes, makeup and so on. Anne had been filling me in with the kind of back-to-back personal detail that left no room for pause. There was Joan's knowledge of lighting, stage position, sound. Her authority around the selection of a particular gown, long or short, backless or full sleeve. 'You're going to need to slow down,' I said. 'If I'm to help in any way, if I'm to come with you, Anne, to Joan Collins' house this evening, without, as far as I can see, a formal invitation. You're going to need to give me more information. I thought you'd signed that book contract ages ago? I thought you were about to deliver?'

Anne sighed, somewhat theatrically. 'Alright then, here—' she turned and in one deft movement removed 'Skip-to-my-Lou' from the table beside her and used the space to spread out a range of pages and photographs taken out of the satchel she'd been wearing over her shoulder all the while. Why hadn't I noticed it? That even at this party Anne had come prepared with a satchel full of Joan? But there she was, the actress, all over the table. Anne pointed out from the pile of images and pages certain papers for my attention, this photo here, notes on the manuscript there. Each print-out was heavily scored over with handwritten scribble, exclamation marks and Post-its; the images, full colour and black and white, taken of the Hollywood star at different stages of her long acting career, also densely marked up with instruction and ideas for cropping and extrusion. The sense of industry, the sheer amount of recalibration that had been involved in transforming at speed the project from one kind of undertaking—a glossy coffee table bio—into another—a densely worded treatise on representation and personality as represented by an actress regarded as both English and American, from both old world and new—was impressive. Anne plucked two fresh glasses from the twinkling choir of flutes that seemed to be in attendance, if you like, to all her hard work. She poured champagne into both of them at great speed, as if it was water, and handed me one of them. 'Have this,' she said. 'I'll tell you everything.'

It turned out that the book she had been working on about 'Joan', as she familiarly referred to her subject, had taken much longer to put together than I'd thought. A project that had started as a simple ghosting exercise—*A Player's Life: In her own words*—something like that—had expanded and grown in ways Anne couldn't quite put her finger on, and it had been the conversation she'd finally had with Joan, just days ago, when the two had finally met and the term 'starlet' was first engaged, that had generated, apparently, a change of direction, of focus, of heart. Up until then, the emails, the interviews … The book that had been commissioned seemed to be the book that was taking shape. I'd heard all about it from Anne's partner, Caroline, who had told me that for some time she had been having to sit short written tests on 'Joan' that had been created and were then assessed by Anne. She was being viva'd by her every Friday evening before supper in order that facts could be checked and timelines tightened. According to Caroline, things had been going pretty smoothly.

Those words 'starlet' and 'actress', though, had entered that calm world of Socratic dialogue and blown wide open what turned out to be volatile research material. Anne was going on and on about it. 'Starlet *turned* actress, see?' she kept repeating, now italicising the verb for emphasis and gesturing wildly with her glass. 'Turned … *Turned*, Mary. The one *turned* into the other.' 'But aren't they both,' I ventured at last, 'the same thing?' I would have quite liked another glass of champagne. Just to sit back, be a guest, enjoy the roses. Not to have to necessarily concentrate, or, right now, even think about Joan Collins. 'You know,' I mumbled, 'starlet first, actress later. That was Marilyn Monroe, too, and, um …' I finished lamely, 'lots of people …'

'Nonsense!' Anne was magnificent. In one swift motion she seized in both hands the bowl of 'Old Glory' that had been placed next to me and put it down on the floor between us. Now she could gesture more freely. 'We're imagining not just a book but the description of a whole form of representation here,' she said, lifting up her arms and making a large circular shape in the air with her hands. 'A Greek Theatre, only more ancient than Euripides, Aeschylus … Because this theatre Joan shows us is the theatre that is all around, you see?' She indicated the brightly lit room, the people gathered, the walls enclosing us all against the quantities of the night. 'You see the circle,

Mary? The circus?' She was exultant. 'And Joan is here, right here in the centre, in the centre of the stage,' she indicated 'Old Glory' between us. 'And here we are, too, you and I, we are the chorus, we are stepping into the circle with her ... Come!' Anne took my hand and stepped back, raising both our arms in a triumphant salute. 'Biography—bollocks!' she cried out. 'A dress is NEVER just a dress!'

There was a dangerous tinkle of crystal, and she turned in the nick of time to steady the tray of flutes shimmering behind her. 'Forget about biography,' she went on. 'This book about Joan Collins is to be a living text, Mary. Something that affects us all. The idea of playing one's part, acting out ... Girl into Actress. Woman into Queen. That's the thing which is on,' she paused, wittily, 'show here. That's the story. And that old idea of personal history? Of an individual self and one old emotion after the other, all the post-Freud rubbish? I am not interested in that. And neither,' she finished, 'is Joan'. She looked at me triumphantly. 'I know it,' she said. 'I just have to find a way of telling her so.' Anne paused then, her head slightly to one side, as if to consider her words, but in fact it was for dramatic effect. Her voice had been raised and compelling; she now dropped it to a whisper. 'I am forming here a non-narrative—or at least in the terms that we think of as narrative.' She smiled secretively. 'It's a kind of instruction I am shaping instead, to reposition the story of Joan as a set of principles for being in the world. For life. Give me your glass.' She stepped neatly across 'Old Glory' and lunged for one of the bottles there on the table in the corner. 'It's going to be amazing.' She swished champagne again into both of our empty flutes and raised them. 'A toast,' she said. 'To you and me. Come on.' She passed me my glass. 'Drink up. I'm taking you to meet Joan so you can tell her what we've done with her book. Cheers!'

'Hang on—'. What was that? *Me* tell? What *we've* done?

'Cheers!' Anne said again.

I suppose, if I'd been more realistic about Anne's enthusiasm to come with me to Marjorie's launch, I might have known something of this sort was in the air. Anne is always totally focused on the projects she has in hand and has no interest in diversions; most certainly she has no interest in the historic rose gardens of England. These new ideas of hers about Joan Collins that were being formulated, distinctions made between the self and its projection, between interior being and outward show, fact and art, starlet and actress and the vast existential and ancient space that exists between the two, were a result of recent days of fiendish study. Her presence, then, at a party, at this point in the proceedings, was by no means random. Caroline wasn't there, was she? That was because Caroline would have been needed at home and right now was itemising, no doubt, all manner of detail that up until then had been only background information but was now the very content of Anne's project. Caroline's, then, were the lists of chiffon gowns, of tights and hairdressers; Caroline herself the necessary and fundamental provider of the freshly vital stuff of theatre and performance which Anne would subsequently mash-up in her clever, highly theorised post-structurally educated way and turn into new concept chapters and close readings. There was no time, for Caroline, for parties. While Anne … Anne was here because of this meeting she'd organised, with which I'd become most definitely 'involved'. Anne was here, at Marjorie's, because of some get-together that had been arranged in which she was going to tell the actress what she'd done with her 'Life'—not ghosted it at all but created from it that 'living text' as she'd reminded me as we finished our champagne. Only she wasn't to tell Joan Collins. I was. The whole thing had been planned in advance that I might now be part of the production.

There was the sound of a spoon, then, a tapping at the edge of a crystal glass. Marjorie was getting ready to make a speech. The room went quiet. 'Good evening, everyone ...'

'Just remember, starlet *turned* actress is key,' Anne whispered fiercely in my ear. 'And to see within that, *within* that ...'

'A life performance,' I murmured.

'EXACTLY!' Anne drained her glass. Her voice had rung out in the silence. 'I KNEW you would understand.' Everyone had turned from Marjorie to look over at us, where we stood, somewhat cramped behind the sofa, roses pushed away from the table to make room for the piles of papers, roses on the floor. Anne reverted to her stage whisper, 'Glamorous person becomes powerful impersonator. You've followed the thinking through and caught up completely.'

'It's the story of all of us,' I managed, under my breath, without seeming to move my lips. How impolite it was to be carrying on this way, talking about these things while Marjorie was introducing herself and her own book. So very impolite. 'Only Joan's the extreme example,' I finished in a ventriloquist's rush. 'She's the paradigm for—'

'That's it,' Anne was satisfied. 'A life performance. You've got it in one.'

'I want to say a few words,' Marjorie was now starting her speech. Her guests had turned back to face her, all rapt attention. I looked at them, at the group gathered around their hostess author, at the beautiful room, the flower arrangements everywhere ... Whose house was this anyway? An elegant townhouse in the middle of Mayfair? It had to be someone connected to historic rose gardens of England for it was surely not where Marjorie lived. For a second, I wondered if even this, our being here, might be part of Anne's planning, too, that we, right now, might be standing in the drawing room of Joan

Collins' Mayfair home and already in the middle of that performance, in the scene that was to follow this. But no, 'First of all, thank you to William and Helen for providing this lovely setting,' Marjorie was saying, 'and to you all for coming …'

How lovely it was. Or seemed. Or both. Is what I was thinking. As though I was noticing the space around me for the first time, the roses as though just placed there this second for effect, and the glasses; the light, the fragrance … The very air seemed ringed by the sense of occasion, everything arriving together into the singular moment of the present tense, as though each detail of what Marjorie was telling us, about the Middle Ages and about England and about love and gardens and traditions and roses, marked out precisely in her consonants and syllables the very seconds and minutes of our shared lives together.

Anne's head was down; she was texting.

'And the rose itself resembles a kind of early medieval lyric,' I heard. 'A composition that will come to be played out in certain fourteenth-century knot gardens and border arrangements and seen later in the walled enclosures of the first flowering of renaissance …'

'Right.' Anne pocketed her phone. 'That's done.' She was still whispering, though far too loudly. 'Come on,' she said. 'Her PA's just texted me. It's a good time to go round there. Joan goes to bed early. It's brilliant that we were able to meet here at Marjorie's because it's only a couple of streets away. We can walk.'

I shook my head, made a gesture, *shhh*, and indicated towards Marjorie. She was still speaking. Anne, beautifully brought up as she had been, knew enough not to bolt at that second. But the minute the applause sounded—Marjorie had finished her speech with the phrase 'and here we are!' and everyone was clapping and calling 'hurrah!'—we did. We bolted. We left that drawing room of roses for another, just as fair, and with a rose of its own set in among it, coiffed and made-up and resplendent in pink satin, as old, you might say, as time itself, and every bit as compelling.

I repeat here—for repetition, yes, the chant of it, its rhythm and sound, is crucial in any drama—all this was only two weeks ago. And life, as I say, has adjusted itself dramatically since; the articulated days and weeks of experience shaped into another representational form to my mind now thoroughly disconnected from that other subjective reading of experience from which crude biography may be fashioned. For as I did indeed meet the subject of Anne's study that night, as I was most surely 'rolled out'—as Anne put it later, 'it was brilliant the way I rolled you out. Just when I could see Joan was flagging, on the history of rhetoric and choreographed action and all that, you came in with that word of yours and it spurred the whole thing on'—so too was I changed by that same meeting and my own role in it. Though Joan herself, of course, barely needed any telling. All Anne's concern around pitching to her a reimagined concept for the book? All my worry about being there in the first place and having to speak? It was as if the principal actor in our drama was already on the stage, waiting for us. After we'd finished with our pitch and I'd completed my part, she drew both of us close, extending her hands to us as we stood, like acolytes, on either side of her, to bring us towards her so that we might kiss her on the cheek. A kind of ceremony had been enacted there, in her home. A cycle that she had set in motion—most surely set, when she delivered her life story to Anne as the subject for a book in the first place—completed.

Now her biographer could move on. The starlet-turned-actress' response and actions would lead straight back to Anne's agent for the reissue of the book's contract in line with the new approach that would take a reader from those first early black-and-white days of a young woman in a spangled playsuit to the late highly glossed images of a goddess in pure white at the turn of a new century all indicated by a special frontispiece to be created by the subject herself, framed in the language of Aristotle and ancient Greek tragedy, about the endless and necessarily primitive cycle of birth and death represented as a series of performances, of actions as presentation, as example, of theatre as life. As Joan had said, 'It's all example, darlings,' giving us one of her ravishing smiles. 'All of it,' she said. 'The whole damn, lovely thing. We're just one marvellous piece of show-and-tell after another.'

And what was that word I'd thought to use? Had the wit to insert, in the conversation that had taken place during a meeting that had been arranged for that evening after Anne and I had bolted from Marjorie's rose-filled party and were rushing, speed-walking, through the early summer's dark towards the home of an actress I'd never given much thought to before then? What was it, I was still trying to figure, as Anne and I stood outside in the street after our meeting with Joan, the 'book in the bag' as Anne said, but neither of us quite able to believe the whole construction of events had ended up being, despite its complexity, so simple? What word?

'Oh, I remember!' It came back to me.

'Exactly!' Anne said. We were still standing there, the two of us in Belgrave Square, as though we never wanted to leave, looking back up at the window of a certain beautifully lit drawing room, the outline of an actress, that stage figure, placed somewhere, poised, within it. The night was warm. The rest of the house, the terrace, was in darkness, but still, there was that one particular and lovely illumination, that square of light, that bright theatre, in the deep infinity of the sky.

'Listen,' Anne said. 'You should write a story about all this. Now that we're quite clear, I mean, about Joan.' It was an ending of sorts she was indicating, we both knew that, but containing within it my own understanding of practice and performance which was only just beginning.

'You definitely should,' Anne said again. 'A short story. All about what we've learned of the world and of life and the part we play in the larger drama of experience and why Joan Collins is important.'

I nodded.

'And that fancy word—'

'Yep.' I knew exactly where she was going with this.

'That word can be part of its title,' Anne finished.

Wairarapa

B eulah came in most weekends with her sweets and those presents but who cared about that because none of the cousins believed the presents were real. So there were foil papers. And ribbons sometimes. So the presents got wrapped. The paper was crumpled and there was no tape. Those presents were bundled, they were stolen. Beulah saying, 'Here you kids'—and giving them out like she was some kind of aunt and not just a skinny little girl who'd stick a needle into her own ears to pierce them. Ronnie said she wasn't going to accept any of Beulah's stuff, not the sweets either. Ronnie was the eldest Mason; her mother and the Cannons' and the MacFarlanes' mothers had been sisters once.* 'Jesus,' said Ronnie. 'That stuff Beulah sucks on would rot enamel clean off.'

Still, the presents were there, and you couldn't say they weren't new. Not real, maybe—but in their packets. The paper doll books and embroidery sets. 'All of it! All of it!' sang little Lizzie, 'thieved and bad.' 'Don't cut the dolls out then,' said Martin. 'Give them back.' But Beulah would be gone by then, returned to where she came from, and the dolls had pretty clothes to wear.

Because that kid? She only stayed at the grandmother's one or two nights at most. She couldn't be a cousin. The cousins were all 'under one roof', that's what their grandmother said, with the mothers up north throwing money away at the racetrack with men. So what was it about Beulah then? If she wasn't relative? Who were her people? What was she doing being among them, those days she came in? The grandmother kept saying Beulah was a cousin, though, just as the rest of them were but it seemed like everything to do with Beulah was connected to a lie. And one thing was for sure: her type was not the sort to have money for presents. With the cheap thin socks and the little outfits that were way too small … She didn't even have a nightdress, Beulah. Yet there she was, trying to please the cousins with sweets and all the rest of it, acting like she was one of them when their mothers didn't have another sister.

But did they? Could you be sure? With their mothers' brother's boy arriving at the grandmother's earlier in the spring, that little thing with his cheek and a surprise, alright, because the mothers hadn't ever talked about a brother or a nephew before. The new brother of the mothers may have been sick with being out of work and never drying out, the grandmother said, but still the figure of him counted as an uncle, which made of the little person he'd brought with him a cousin too. Could that leave more around, then, to be family with? After the queer back slaps coming from the father and his son, their matching suits and 'Great to see yah!' vaudeville cries? For now here was this summer with this Beulah in it. Their grandmother calling her 'my special girl' and saying to the cousins, 'You watch it, you lot. You be nice to Beulah; she's got no one else.' And who were the cousins anyhow, the grandmother said, to think themselves so special? With their mothers all up racing at Waipu and carrying on with men? 'You watch it, alright,' she told them. 'You be nice to Beulah, or when she's gone, I'll skin you alive.'

For sure, for the grandmother, it was as though the cousins were her own children. She'd brought them in under one roof when they needed to be brought in and that had always been her way. Nine of them altogether and ten if you counted the little Raymond because he'd be back soon, the grandmother had said. So that made four Masons, three Cannons, two MacFarlanes and, with the disappeared uncle come back as a Hillyard, a tiny Hillyard cousin … Who might guess what the grandmother would count next as blood? The mothers, after all, were denying themselves as sisters so anything, the cousins knew, anything could be true. There might as well have been only one daughter, is what the mothers said, 'Only one little girl for Daddy.' But you add another, then there's two, three … Why not? It was still the case that only one of them would find herself fit to inherit when their father's lawyer was done. Is how that bad racetrack money had been fixed, the lawyer said. That old Wairarapa fortune. He was busy with it round the clock, he told the grandmother, and had been ever since the funds had been so freshly left. No surprise, then, 'That cat!' the cousins heard. Or 'Bitch'. About a mother, or it might have been two of them speaking about the other. Because if only one could come into the 'estate entire', then of course the sisters would undo their own blood ties to make it come good for all three of them in the end. It's what family did, didn't it? Tell stories? Make sure things would turn out ok? And so by now you might really believe the sisters had never been related either; Ronnie had heard her mother say it enough times. 'I don't have any sisters'—even though she and the cousins kept seeing the three of them together, dressed up and going out, while the same mother was also saying to Ronnie that she might have had sisters once, 'But not anymore, baby girl, and don't you forget it.' So it was the case then, it had to be, that you couldn't be sure about a mother. Or the others. And the grandmother would never say. But what you did know was that the numbers could go to eleven just like that if you counted Beulah and who was counting her? The lawyer? Could he?

Would he? Count someone who came prancing in on a Saturday in a nylon party dress and shoes that didn't fit but was gone by Sunday night? Someone who might try to act like she was family but who talked all the time, and way too much, pressing up to the cousins and wanting to show them things, this part of her body or that—'Look at this rash on my belly, see? These burn marks that itch?'—giving out presents and trying to hold hands afterwards and be far, far too close. And would then leave. Disappeared as fast from the grandmother's house when her own strange mother came by to fetch her, someone 'equally, equally,' said Ronnie, 'skinny and white.' And, behind her back in a whisper, 'That mother of Beulah's is a *tart.*'

Tart! Ronnie figured she was white enough. Like the sun never got to her. Did that make her one? That even in the middle of a long dry summer it was as though a so-called mother had never put a skinny foot outside? Maybe, maybe. Because—Tart! Or 'Something', Ronnie said. 'Or someone ...' She always had opinions. 'Has got to her.' The mother had the skinny legs of a tart, said Ronnie. And her knees with scabs on, just like young Martin, like she was some kind of kid herself because she would pick at them while talking to the grandmother, eyeing up the cousins. 'You got all of them, Mother? You got all them all at once?' Then later, when she was about to leave with Beulah, saying—trying to suck up, Ronnie said—'You kids had a good time today? You like those things Beulah brought you? That sewing crap? The thing with felt? You like that stuff, she'll give you more of those good presents, Beulah will. You play your cards right I'll bring her back next week, and now you say bye to your Aunty Pat.' And, 'That's your Aunty Pat speaking to you,' the grandmother would say then, because the cousins ... well ... none of them had replied with a single word.

'But-But-But …' Carol couldn't say it fast enough, once those two had left and the cousins were on their own again. 'She can't be an aunt. She can't be.' Though thinking at the same time, maybe, about her own two because, Aunt Billie and Fran, if they were no longer supposed to be sisters then what put Carol in such a position to have opinions about aunts? Sisters didn't do what those two did, that's what her mother said to Carol, when she was all for not wanting to see the others ever again. Putting her lipstick on in front of the mirror and pressing her lips on a tissue to leave the red kiss of her mouth right there. 'Who needs them?' she might say to Carol, 'I don't.' Only then, as Carol also saw, as the cousins had seen on repeat these past months, they would all get together again, the three of them, talking odds as usual, and form and line and how to win. Didn't matter how many lipstick kisses they'd left on tissues, they'd be off and away when there was some money around and a horse they wanted to follow. Did they have shares in some bloodstock, even? Martin had suggested it. Some bit of leftover divorce settlement from one of them, maybe, or part payment, why not, of that bad inheritance released up front and gone into some colt or brood-mare, or even two? Carol was apt to consider herself someone who would think such matters through, the family's money and where it came from, where it was going. She was the sort of cousin who would want to speak right back to the grandmother about something that felt like it was only made up for the sake of a fact having to account for itself, 'the right breeding for the right race', as her mother had always told her life should be. 'I don't like her,' is what Carol said straight out about the mother of Beulah when the subject of a new aunt came up again. 'She smells,' said Peter, Carol's brother after all so of course he would join in to back her, along with Felicity, her favourite girl cousin, with something of her own to say. 'Oh get your five cents in,' the grandmother said. 'You want a good slap, the lot of you, you spoilt brats. Your mothers need whipping as well.' And the cousins might look at each other then. For who was the grandmother that she would take sides against them? And next thing she said, 'You all need to learn to be kind.'

God's Truth in Heaven! 'Kind'? What was that supposed to mean? The cousins couldn't believe what they were hearing. What could be happening and all at once that a situation might change so fast with just one sentence, one word—that the grandmother might be right? To bring in this new idea of 'kinship', Ronnie said was another word related to 'kind'. 'Like kin—see?' Ronnie said. 'Kind.' There'd never been that sort of talk before. That the smell was the perfume Beulah's mother used, the grandmother said, and just because it wasn't nice didn't mean it wasn't something that poor young woman hadn't tried with; that the cousins should make an effort to understand. 'You kids don't know who you are talking about,' the grandmother said, and she turned away from them, walked straight out of the kitchen, down the hall and through the open door. And alright, then. The cousins decided on the spot. Because maybe they didn't. Ronnie was the first to organise a meeting about it in her room. 'Get in here now,' she said to the rest of them, the oldest after all so of course she would be in charge with the Masons' whole bedroom become her own and the big flowery curtains drawn closed against the brightness of the day. The cousins could only sit on her bed and on Lizzie's and Martin's or on the floor while she spoke, using these new words of hers in her own arrangement, telling them that maybe now was the time to know some more about Beulah, to get to know, to under-stand. 'I didn't use to think this way,' said Ronnie. 'But now, well ... with things becoming different from how they used to be ... I do.'

And, so. Okay. Well, yes, alright then, the cousins thought. Maybe they needed to start seeing things Ronnie's way too ... With the ground slipping away from under them, is how it felt, they all agreed—the grandmother's new way of talking causing a shake, and suddenly you thought you might fall. So, alright, they said back to her, they decided. Better say yes, then. For kin. And yes, too, alright, for kind. You might have thought what could 'kind' possibly have to do with the grandmother but here it was with them now, that word—so better learn from it and hang on to the grandmother for all they were worth. 'A resilient woman,' as Ronnie put it, another word learned at that fancy boarding school of hers. 'There's nothing our grandmother doesn't know about, hasn't thought about,' Ronnie said. She was lounging against the doorjamb of the Mason bedroom as she spoke, taller than the rest by far and smoothly calm in her blue uniform jumper with its golden crest, a thing she liked to wear on cold days. 'She's incorporated us all,' Ronnie said. She put her long arms up to reach the top of the door ledge, touching it that easily it wasn't even stretching. 'Think about it,' she said. And so the cousins did, sitting there, all of them quiet, not moving, while Ronnie tiptoed her fingers along the ledge looking down at them. For there she was, the grandmother. As though standing right behind Ronnie, that same resilient woman. Speaking for Beulah. Speaking for Beulah's mother too. In the same way, when you came to consider it, she'd spoken for that brother and his connected child. The numbers, Ronnie showed them, for the grandmother, could easily grow.

'Even though I'm certain our mothers wouldn't know someone like Beulah's mother ...' That was Mary, first to say something to break the silence, second of the Cannons after Carol and the prettiest of the girls. 'I also know a resilient woman might think our mothers are—' Martin interrupted her, 'You mean bad?' 'After all, we don't know who they're seeing up there, where they are now,' Ronnie reminded him. She was still lounging against the doorway, her jersey fitting her exactly in every smooth place. 'Jesus,' said Peter. 'We know damn squit,' said little Lizzie. 'Well, we might try,' finished Dan. He put his thumb back in his mouth after that because he was only four and still sucked it.

'Jesus,' again, then. For Ronnie was right. The cousins had better say yes for resilient, too. Just as for kind. And for kin. Kinship. These words had to apply. Because the grandmother had something she was keeping from them and was using her great strength to do so—they were getting to the enormity of that knowledge pretty fast. Some kind of history, information about the family, not just about the mothers but these others who acted as though they were familiar. From the uncle and his strange son—and something there to do with a boy that little person had managed to hurt—and now this Pat and Beulah ... What kind of people were these? Where had they come from? Nothing was as it should be. And how else, the cousins were starting to think, might things change? That there were other things going to be emerging now, that would arise? Everyone starting to wonder—like why Ronnie was at that fancy school when their mothers never cared about that sort of thing. 'What's that about, eh?' asked Martin on more than one occasion, after the grandmother had made reference to all of their education and what money might be used for what cousin and whose choice that would be—this new way of her talking that had come out of another remark to do with Beulah and how the rest of them could compare. 'I can turn it all around, you know,' the grandmother had said. 'Switch it on or off. You should remember that. Your mothers should remember it, too.' She seemed to be not interested at all in the cousins as she spoke, looking out the open window, thinking about something else that had nothing to do with them, they could see it in her face. That she was planning something. Figuring it through. And so their situation might not necessarily continue in the same way after this summer's end, is how Martin saw it. Like Ronnie might not get to stay on and board, that maybe all of them would be moved out of their schools. Dan lifted from his special little kindy, and then where would he go …

And would the mothers even come back from Waipu? Now that Beulah's visits seemed fixed the cousins were starting to feel anything was possible, anything. Though the mothers had always returned in time for the new term before … still, 'Your life not so pretty as you might think,' the grandmother had said once after Beulah had been in, another of those scary remarks rising like fresh landscape around them, causing the ground to shift. 'What do you mean? What do you mean?' That was little Lizzie bouncing, wanting all knowledge. 'Nothing. Be quiet. Cut out your dolls.'

It was by now the case for the cousins for sure that everything seemed to be like secrets, secrets, and their own mothers who were supposed to be parents, relations, adults … All of them in on it like a gang gone haywire with betting and never telling what the odds were, how it could come right. Ten of them relative, and eleven if you counted Beulah—though the cousins were still asking, did she count, did she? As blood? When blood stayed with you, didn't it? You didn't get the choice of days? Whereas that Beulah disappeared as fast when her strange mother, who was not like a mother but more like a sister of Beulah, showed up at the house. And again, 'That's your Aunty Pat speaking,' the grandmother would say to the cousins—they were sulking around on the sofas in the sitting room, waiting for their favourite programmes to come on TV. 'You go through and talk to her. You listen to her and be polite.' 'But,' said Felicity, emboldened, 'I really don't believe she's relative.' 'Otherwise,' pressed Carol, straight to the grandmother's face, 'why doesn't Beulah fully stay?' 'She smells,' said Mary. 'That's just the perfume her mother uses, dummy,' the grandmother said. 'I told you that already. You be kind. Pat's grandmother helped me when I first came here as a bride. That woman lived next door and she was my only, my dearest friend.'

The cousins stopped what they were doing then. 'Eh?' said Peter. He sat up. For how could that sentence fit into anything that was real? That Pat had had a grandmother who could have been the grand-mother's friend? The grandmother had never had any friends, only family. So what was that about? And that she would know someone like Pat's grandmother in the first place …. What was going on? And then there was the other fact, too, of 'bride'? They'd never heard the grandmother talk about being married before. Plus, that house next door was empty and always had been. They owned it, didn't they? Just like they owned all the land around here? So how were they supposed to believe now that this Pat had somehow been connected to it, to have had a grandmother who had lived right here where they lived? The cousins looked at each other. It was just like Peter said. 'Eh?' As though they had no manners, realising, and fully by now, that they didn't have the first idea about the grandmother. 'What do you mean?' said Peter—because of course certain things the grand-mother had always kept hidden away, you could find bits of them, like photos and jewels, in cupboards, in boxes and in little wooden drawers that used to have a lock, you could see the places that took a key. But here she was now, telling them about being a bride and about Pat's grandmother who used to live here being her friend, someone who had had a young daughter, the grandmother said, who would babysit their mothers when they were little but who was growing up and so the mother and her daughter had had to move away. 'It was a great sadness to me when Pat's grandmother left the Wairarapa,' she said. At which point the cousins couldn't even react for the shock of hearing again that those sorts of people could have had anything to do with their mothers … Even been here in the first place … For how could it be? Any of it? How?

And there was their own grandmother. She was looking out the window, more and more become as though someone they'd never known. 'I always thought I would be able to help her here,' she was saying. 'I did. Despite everything. In the same way that I help with all of you.' She turned around then, to face them. 'You see?' she said. But no! The cousins didn't see! That someone like Pat had had a grandmother who had been part of the grandmother's life, and this before any of their own mothers had even been born … In this part of the country that had only ever held their family, only them … No! Because how could that be? When this place, all of it, its land and skies and the grandmother's house and the old racetrack on the edge of town had only ever been somewhere for their family, for the cousins and the grandmother and the mothers. Again no! Nor that the grandmother would not keep these details packed away as she usually did, along with the other ideas about herself—those dresses she used to wear before she came here, to this part of the country, the big rooms behind her in the photos, with pictures on the walls and mirrors and twinkling lights—but was letting it out now to show. What was happening? What was going on? 'I was the one who told her to get away from here as far as she could,' the grandmother was saying, more to herself than to the cousins, in a kind of a dream, the light from the open window only increasing the light already around her, talking about a time long ago and that since then she knew nothing about her, the 'dear, dear friend', just nothing … Or did she? For now here was that woman's granddaughter after all. And here as well was this Beulah.

Days went on after that, and more days. Nothing so special in the end, the cousins were coming to register for themselves, that it wouldn't be open like a box to change. And yes, of course you might say the grandmother was a resilient woman, and a resilient woman would have private information about herself just as their own parents did—ganging around together and losing money on the races and never telling the cousins anything. But what was starting to emerge now was clearly part of a story that came from way beyond the grandmother's house and garden and the town, and was different, all different, from the made-up stuff the cousins were used to. Like Felicity had heard about Uncle Ross Cannon with a filly due to be ridden later in the summer before school went back, and her mother had said they might all go down to Invercargill with him and watch her win. Only that was never going to happen because Uncle Ross, the grandmother told them, was a fantasist and a fool. All of her daughters, all three of them, she said, had married bad men. And she'd never talked before about the mothers' lives that way. It was terrifying and new, this bringing of a past into the present—as though whole mountains were rising up for the cousins, a rushing river of new ideas about their family tumbling along and it could cause landslides, slipping in the mud and going under. Though the grandmother hadn't told them any more … still, 'Wastrels,' she said. 'You're damn lucky, you kids, your mothers have had the sense to let you come and live with me when they can't manage on their own. When they go off and act up and carry on the way they do. You be glad they feel they can leave you here with me. Not everyone, you know, is so able.'

The cousins felt far, far away from the grandmother by then. It seemed that they could barely hear her voice. Autumn was coming. It was in the distance, as though heading their way from a part of the country they'd never visited before and didn't want to. A place that was all questions with no answers, caught up in that land of hills and miles that lay beyond the window, beyond the garden and the old

track and the horses and the paddocks and the green ... Because what
did the grandmother mean now with that 'able'? Able to do what?
Be a family? Let other family in? They really had better look wise,
they said. Ronnie was right. They were all of them thinking about it,
and talking, they couldn't stop, whispering in each other's rooms at
night. They decided that for good or bad they had better understand,
and fast, all of them together, how Beulah had brought out a side of
their situation that they'd thought, as far as their grandmother was
concerned at least, was fixed. For who was looking over what might
happen here? With this new landscape opened up around them, 'a
place of fissures and ravines' is how Ronnie described it. And how
long could it last? Their protected living with their grandmother?
Their own way of being cousins and being able? That they could stay
here when they needed, when the aunts and their husbands were not
around? The presents of Beulah and her loud calls, that tiny man's
arrival back in the spring for two days, nothing compared to what was
happening now, just nothing, with this shift in the balance of secrets
kept and stories told ... A new kind of past being given up and set
in motion—Beulah wanting to hold the cousins' hands in her tight,
dry little grip and tell them things they didn't want to hear about her
and her strange life, pulling up her sleeves to show them her eczema,
her infected skin, acting like she knew them so well—'Come here
you kids, I've got something else for you', rattling in a plastic bag
for more presents—and cuddling up to the grandmother when no
one cuddled up to the grandmother and there was the grandmother
allowing it, stroking her hair ... The cousins couldn't figure any of it.
Carol couldn't, for all the ideas she wanted to express. Felicity said
Beulah had been in care; she'd overheard the grandmother on the
phone. That Beulah was an orphan, then, just as Beulah was a thief.
'In care' meant borstal, a prison, kind of, but worse because it was
for kids. You could hear the awfulness of it in the very word. Borstal.

'Jail for children,' Peter said. 'Think what kind of children they must be ...'

He might have said more but the grandmother had come into the MacFarlanes' room where the cousins had gathered to talk about the most recent visit and had heard him. 'Listen,' she grabbed Peter's ear and twisted it like he was a little piglet she'd never liked. 'Far as I'm concerned your cousin's the same as you, as you all are. You got that? I hear another mean word from you, and I'll twist this ear of yours right off your head. I'll stick the lot of you in the motel down the highway to live on beer and chips and see how you like it. Now scoot. Next week, when Beulah's here, I'm taking all of you uptown to the village for tea and cakes, and you'll behave nicely, you'll be a family to her, you will, or I'll send you all back, the job lot of you, and keep Beulah to myself.'

Was how things might well finish up, too, the cousins could guess. Could hear it in the grandmother's voice, could see it in the expression on her face. There was that ravine. There were those fissures. Step by step they were coming to realise for themselves—with their eldest cousin looking on at them from where she'd lounged in the doorway that day and who had known about it first—how not being certain about their family was the only certain thing about it. All ten cousins, from little clever Dan right through to Ronnie herself and including the tiny man who'd hurt a child, Beulah said, and had used a knife to get money and was a bully and a thief, but even so with the Hillyard name attached ... All of us in the end coming to know the truth about Beulah and about blood, the generation of it that was not just horses and racing but the sort of relatives we came from. The story of our own bad bloodline, you might say—showing up first in one careful step after another and then breaking into a run of galloping anxiety and fear of where it might lead us, the whip of our questions getting us to the end of the racetrack of that summer, hurtling towards it and not wanting to … But getting there even so—to an understanding of a history we were coming to see and hope against but then would know for sure as the full account of what had happened to our family, to all of us… Because of what had happened first to the grandmother's friend.

And it was Wairarapa alright. Oh yes. Closed in like a box, maybe, that had not been opened but was open now and showing itself, showing itself still … Starting before the grandmother came here, and going on … Before our grandmother knew about it, even. Before she had even had a friend who used to live next door. In the same way as it then went on to happen to that same friend's daughter, and then, in turn, to her daughter's daughter … and … and … who knew? How many years it might continue? Long lines of wrongful breeding, and for long years of a life and for more … So that, without it having a beginning and a middle and an end, without being entirely sure of how the details might fit, how it was exactly that the grandmother would play her part—she the only one here in this story after all who by blood was not connected—still the truth showed up as a realisation we arrived at, of how everything came together, was connected. And, as Ronnie said, 'Be careful here. Be very careful.' For how close did we come? The cousins? To being caught up in the same aftermath caused by that old husband of our grandmother, that old daddy? Close enough. I felt the prickle of it on my own skin.

'Just be glad he stopped wanting to live here,' Ronnie said. 'That he moved far away when our own mothers were still really little.' For she might have been resilient, our grandmother, 'resilient' remember? Ronnie's word? But it was only luck, you might say, and wanting other things for himself that had stopped him coming back, that man, to where he was from; this place his own family's land after all.

'So you see?' said Ronnie. 'You see?' How close he could have been? That though the grandmother would have taken some kind of action against him for sure, Ronnie told us—when she realised the sort of husband she had married—it might not necessarily have prevented him deciding to come back to be near where his wife still lived with their three daughters, in his own home town, and use that old bad thoroughbred money of his to stay. 'Thank God none of us knew him,' was what Ronnie said. It made me remember how she herself had looked that day, leaning up against the outline of an open door showing in the smoothness of her dark blue jersey all of her own new and lovely shape. 'Because think about it,' she said. And we were. We were all of us thinking by then not only about our mothers and who their father had been. We were thinking about Pat. And we were thinking about Beulah, too.

It was in the spirit of a full and exact conclusion then, though at the time we didn't know how it would come together exactly, with the estate finally settled for the mothers not just in three but, for the reasons of my grandmother's great resilience, for five, and with everyone really knowing, after wondering about it, I suppose, for years, and fearing for all that time that he might return some day, that the old man had well and truly died, the horses run their course and their bright colours taken down—that we did indeed go uptown to the village the following Saturday, as our grandmother had said we would, this, the last time that poor Beulah would come in. And everyone put on something. The grandmother, the pretty shoes with the heels and her straw summer hat. The boys, their school shirts and wetting down their hair, even Peter did it. And little Dan was got out of his overalls and into a dress of mine cut down to fit him that he loved to wear, the other girls with ribbons, and Felicity in the glittery barrette with diamonds we all wanted. Beulah herself was enabled. There she was that day in a matching ensemble her mother had been able to find, a skirt and top that fitted her at last and with its own jacket even, it had half sleeves. 'You're pretty enough, you see,' said the grandmother, when she'd finished brushing silkily and tying back in a ponytail Beulah's scrappy hair. 'It was good of you, Pat,' she'd said earlier before that strange young person left again and would return only one more time for Beulah, for this was the end of there being any more cousins. 'To think of providing the girl,' said our grandmother, as she'd looked at Pat, and then across us all, taking in with her one look all twelve of us, cousins, 'with that fresh gingham.'

And 'I done it' Beulah grinned, showing her broken yellow teeth. 'I love these lands of yours,' she said to the grandmother, gesturing about at the high street and its shops, the wide footpath giving off at the end of the road to the paddocks and the fields and all the blue sky beyond. 'I seen to your richnesses,' she said, this Beulah, as though she was a grand princess of the world and full of knowledge, the little kid with pus in her ears from the holes she'd made gone septic. 'You've done a great job with them, my lass,' she said to the woman old enough to be her great grandmother you might say, Beulah's own great grandmother's dear and beloved friend. That kid's words so near the truth she was indeed enabled—to say them out loud, the words, for 'kin' for 'kinship', and for 'kind' ... Now that the story is nearly over and you know the sort of man our grandfather was and what our grandmother tried to do to undo—right here in the place where he was from and where you might have thought nothing much could go wrong—some of what he had done, and done, and done. 'I'm going to get them all more stuff, the children,' Beulah said. 'Just watch. There's nothing I wouldn't give to any of them, eh? Just nothing.'

And away she pranced then—is how I'll remember her, all gingham in a matching set and with patent leather shoes, straight into Cloudie's Tea Shop and started ordering up the best things there. Turning to us, the yellow teeth, one of them was broken, calling out 'Choose! Choose!' as we came in behind her and our grandmother beside. Beulah was a thief and had no knickers on but how we followed her that day. As though something had happened to begin to finally change things for us, for the cousins, for all of us— which, in a way, I suppose it had. For there, there was Beulah, calling out, 'You kids, now choose! The grandmother may say she's taking us, but I have my own folding, I can pay. I'll get us milkshakes, any flavour, and for us all! Just choose. Come on here, my children. What do you want? Let me get it for you now.'

🏃

* *A note to the reader: The Wairarapa family is a large and complicated one, even before the details as recorded in this story emerge to complicate it even further. The Grandmother, as she is called, was married to a Hillyard, whose patronym is taken by her husband's son and his son, and perhaps by the Grandmother herself, but otherwise her three daughters go by their own husbands' surnames—Mason, Cannon, McFarlane—as do their children. These cousins, then, are listed as follows: The Masons—Veronica (Ronnie), Martin, Elizabeth (Lizzie) and Dan; The Cannons—Carol, Mary and Peter; The McFarlanes—Felicity and the narrator herself. As you have now read, we also have Pat and Beulah included in this list, along with*

the stepbrother—and perhaps there are further children, though not in this story. It is not known either, whether Pat and Beulah take the Hillyard name. Unlikely, I would have thought. For, to paraphrase 'Wairarapa', these kinds of people, to their cost and our shame—despite everything a Grandmother could do—have been made to disappear.

Dangerous Dog

In a way, I could start this short story with a dream I had last night in which I was attacked by two rogue Labradors who'd seemed sweet at first but then turned mean. This was outside the park where I normally go running—at the gates of that park—and the Labradors went for me right there, one biting my hand, holding on and not letting go, the other mauling at my clothing. I could start with that, I suppose, because the same park features heavily in the story I want to write and it works as a nice 'gateway to narrative'—a phrase Reed has taught me and the kind of thing I come out with now as casually as terms like 'core muscles' or 'aerobic as opposed to muscular fitness', which have been a natural part of my professional vocabulary as a fitness trainer and personal body development coach.

So yes, I could start with that dream, with me reaching down to a pair of dogs who were sitting just inside the gates to the park, just reaching down to pat their soft black heads—and Wham! Just like that, they were onto me, one with my hand in its mouth, the other grabbing on tight to the hem of my jacket. 'Hang on a minute, you two,' I heard myself say, 'this isn't what you're supposed to do. You're Labradors, for goodness' sake.' At which point, hearing myself speak, I woke up.

Of course everyone knows about dreams like this, about Jung and Freud, those old dream counsellors with their unconscious-world this and their myths-and-meanings that. And sure, we all know about the biting dog dream: that it's about either sexual repression or confidence. Or fear of sex. Or too much, or not enough. Whatever. So I suppose it could be that the dream itself might be a little short story if you wanted. It's starting the writing classes that has got me thinking this way. You, whoever you are, are reading now because you like reading, you're used to it—even something like this, a short story from a writing exercise—and you're used to thinking of life in a fictional sort of way; you probably write short stories yourself. But for me, finding meanings in the day-to-day, using them to create a written piece of work … it's weird and it's exciting. Now I think back at so many things that have happened to me and find shapes in those things, patterns. Like how come I went through most of my adult life in and out of relationships when I know I've got my own ways of going about things, always have had, so why should I be surprised those relationships didn't work out? Of course it comes from being a professional athlete, my mother used to say, as well as having my own business and telling people all the time: You've got to do this. You've got to do that.

And here I am, still doing those things—giving the aerobics and weights lessons, signing up new clients for training etc, etc—but also taking writing classes and everything changed for me because of that. And maybe it's what the dream was telling me—reminding me of that connection between life and art. Who knows. All I can say is that when I started this particular homework—the title we were given: 'Something that really happened that has far-reaching consequences'—I just thought, first off: Hey, get the biting dogs in, Kitty. Start with that.

The class I go to isn't strictly short story writing. I should clarify. It's 'Life Writing' with various approaches to prose. We, to quote the course leaflet, 'draw from material that has occurred in the student's life and from that fashion stories and non-fiction articles—"prose artworks"—that both transform the original and stay true to its original shape and turn of events'. Amazing, right? That a class could deliver that kind of result with a bunch of men and women in their thirties to sixties, taking two hours of night school per week to 'hone their writing skills'. Well that's Reed Garner for you, that one man. He developed the course and teaches the whole thirty-two weeks' worth of it, and he knows what he's doing because he is an American short story writer who himself writes from life, creates those 'prose artworks', and though hardly anyone here has heard of him he's quite a big name in the States, with stuff in *The New Yorker* all the time and collections of short fiction. He has won big prizes over there, too, like the MacArthur Foundation and American Pen and the William Faulkner—this information I have at my fingertips, now, you see, and can write about with such authority and ease. I also know that he has taught at Princeton and Yale and is Visiting Professor of Short Fiction at St Hilda's College, Oxford, which is where my mother used to go. So, hey. I guess I was bound to feel a connection. Because my mother was a big presence in my life, I must tell you, massive, and my dad, too, and I miss them both more than I can say.

Still, with all these credentials running from him like water, Reed is a teacher who doesn't make a big deal of any of that side of things. From the outset he said, 'Guys, we're all in this together. Just because you're starter-writers and I've been doing it longer doesn't make me your professor any more than it makes any of you a student. You'll be teaching me easily as much, if not more, than I'll ever be able to show you.' And then he did this thing with his hair—he has super-long hair that's white as white because of being part Native American and he has to keep flipping it back to get it out of his way—flipping it back and then with one hand gathering it up and twisting it into a pretty little rough ponytail or bun, talking all the while. 'So teach me,' he was saying. 'I'll be paying attention to you all.'

For my part, I couldn't listen hard enough, pay attention close enough … 'Reed Garner. Just say his name out loud, Kitty,' I used to murmur to myself as I was walking home, those first few classes. Not even thinking about going for a run or working out. Just going over ideas about fiction instead and prose and Reed Garner, saying his name. One day he cycled past me as I was in this kind of daydream, and when I lunged out of my thoughts to shout 'Hi!' he nearly fell off his bike, took a sort of tumble to avoid hitting me, and we spoke a few words then, he needed to check I was alright, but then went on his way. Already that feels like a long time ago when we sort of crashed into each other like that on the street … but I know it's got nothing to do with my 'gateway' and 'something that really happened that has far-reaching consequences', so I'd better get on with all that now, the story beginning properly here.

Well, I was running, as I do every morning, through the park, coming back around seven, getting to the front gates, and there up ahead I saw … seven o'clock in the morning, remember, a gang of kids, teenagers I thought at first but more like in their early twenties, and they were laughing at something, a shouting and jeering that sounded like a crowd—though I saw when I got closer that there were only four of them. The thing they were all looking down at that was with them was a dog, a pit bull terrier, with a black, flat expression in its eyes, ears back, head down, tail level … He was pretty unhappy, twitching and twisting on a chain because those kids were tormenting him. One was bent over and poking at him with a stick to make him mad, and he was spinning around and snapping at it. Another was yanking on the chain. 'Nah, Rocky!' one of the kids sneered at him and tickled his balls when the chain was pulled back so tight I could see the little dog was nearly choking. 'Yah! Pussy!' the kid said and made to kick him when his friend released his grip.

Now I may be a personal trainer and strong, but actually I'm quite small. And I may be, yes, super-fit, I am, but I wouldn't describe myself as brawny. Still I hate to see a dog being taunted—any animal, but dogs especially. Perhaps that's because I always had dogs as a kid and my parents, when they were still alive, used to take in strays and mutts, 'orphan anything', my mother used to say—I was an orphan myself, you see, and my mother and father took me in—and I'd always thought I'd have a dog one day when I quit the personal training. Anyhow, all this to say that when I saw those kids, young men really, they weren't kids, when I saw them taunting that little dog so that he was snapping and growling and starting to look as if any minute he was going to slip his chain and make a lunge and then there'd be trouble … Well, I saw red.

Professor Garner—just joking, I mean Reed—says we must never use clichés in a story: 'Do anything to avoid 'em, kids,' he says, in his American way. Yet sometimes, like just then, it seems there is no way around them. Because I did … see red. We'd been reading *Jane Eyre* in class, as part of a study of 'the intersection between Life Writing and Fiction' and looking at how that novel by Charlotte Brontë seems for all the world to be just the story of a particular woman's life, a study of Jane, and not the usual kind of book with a plot that has been figured out in advance to make it seem exciting. The red room in that book—it's there towards the beginning when Jane is being punished by her terrible aunt—and the idea that it might surround a person, that colour, might make her see things in a particular way … that detail stayed with me. All that opening section, actually, because I related to it, maybe, with being an orphan too and my parents only adopting me when I was four so I can remember that other part of my life, not in detail, maybe, the orphanage or 'home' as people always called it, but I can remember my mother and father walking towards me that day they came to collect me, and my mother getting down on her knees in front of me and opening her arms and I ran towards her … and I can remember, too, exactly how I felt, being held in her arms that first time … So yes, the early section of *Jane Eyre*, it stayed with me, how it must have been for Jane to have that terrible aunt and not someone like my mother and what it must have been like, growing up so alone … and 'seeing red', well, altogether it seems a likely expression for me to use—cliché or not—when that book had been so clearly in my mind.

I saw red with what those kids were doing. So instead of walking on, as my friend Merrill said I should have—when I phoned to tell her about it afterwards and she shouted at me, 'Christ, Kit. What were you thinking? That dog was dangerous! Those young men themselves are dangerous! You could have been attacked!'—instead of ignoring the whole situation and just going on my way, I went straight up to those boys, young men, whatever, and said, 'What on earth are you doing?'

Let me tell you, that was a moment. A moment, right then, of silence. Then one of the men said, 'Fuck off, bitch,' and the one beside him, 'Yeah. Fuck off,' and then someone else said, in a low and dangerous voice, 'Get her, Rocky. Get her—' and the dog turned.

Now again, as I say, I'm not tall and what do I know? And I'm not brawny in any way and I'm not confrontational with strangers, but neither do I believe anyone is inherently mean, human or animal, boy or dog … I just don't. It's like bodies. You can be overweight or your tone can be shot to hell or you've got no endurance, no core strength … but I can work with you on that. Take my classes and you'll see, straight away, how together we can improve things. I'm saying all this as a kind of metaphor, I guess I know to call it that now, as a way of showing that I wasn't about to walk away from that situation, even though the boy who held the dog lengthened the chain and the dog lit out at me and someone said 'Get her, Rocky' again, but then the boy with the chain pulled it back just in time, so that nothing happened, even though the little guy's teeth were bared and his eyes like a shark because he was ready to get me alright, he'd been commanded.

'You're being very cruel to that dog,' I said then. 'How old are you all, anyway? Twenty? Thirty? You should know better. Here ...' and at that point I got down on my knees, just like my mother got down on her knees that day at the orphanage, and the little dog looked at me, and his expression changed. His ears went up. He put his head on one side.

'Look at him,' I said to the boys, for now I could see that they were just boys, I'd kind of made that up about them being twenty or thirty, just to flatter them because they wanted to be very, very tough. 'Look,' I said again, from down there, though one of them was lashing some other chain he had, and another was muttering over and over in a dark low voice, 'Fuck, fuck, fuck, fuck, fuck,' just like that, and another turned to spit.

'Look,' I said again, for the third time. And then I put out my balled fist and the dog stretched his head towards me. Then he took a step or two, his head still tilted to one side, while all the time I kept my fist in front of him, quite steady. Then he let out a little whimper and sat down. He had a lovely face. His eyes, which had been black and scary-flat like a killer fish, were now full of thoughts and interest. He gave a little bark, like a puppy. He was really just a puppy. He put out his head towards my hand and smelled it all over and then he licked it. And I opened my hand then to let him sniff my palm and then, when he'd done that, too, I gave him a bit of a scratch around his ears and fondled his muzzle.

'There,' I said to him, and sort of to the boys as well. 'There, you see? Everything's alright.'

The boys kind of shuffled, reassembled slightly. The one in control, using the chain as a lead, just let the chain hang.

'You see,' I said, 'you think you've got a mean dog here, boys. But—' I wasn't looking at them as I spoke. I was just looking at the dog—'he's not mean at all.'

'He should be fucking mean,' said one of them, the one who had been swinging the other length of chain attached to his jeans, though he wasn't swinging it now. 'He should fucking be.'

'But he's not, Steve,' said the boy holding the actual dog chain. 'Look at him. He's a pussy. He's a mummy's dog.'

'My old mum wouldn't be seen dead with a dog like that,' the third boy said. 'She wouldn't be seen dead.'

'His name's not even Rocky,' I said then. 'It's Mr Rochester. Little Roc, for short, because look, he's only a puppy …' By now the boys could see that their dog had his tail wagging, was only wanting to play. Not the kind of dog they'd thought he was at all. 'He's named after a guy I've been reading about in this book about someone's life,' I said. 'That guy is a bit like this dog of yours. He may seem all tough and mean but really …' And I gave Little Roc a lovely rub all over his haunches and down his back. 'Really,' I said, 'this little guy wants—like all of us want—like you boys yourself want …'—and by now I had a puppy snuggled up right by me, his eyes closed with pleasure—'someone to give him attention and to love him and to love them back.'

'Hah!' they all went then, the four kids, and snorted like young ponies.

'You be some crazy bitch,' one of them said, the third one again.

'Well, this book I've been reading, that I was telling you about, *Jane Eyre* ... She seems crazy too, I suppose. But her story is not so different from Mr Rochester here, this little guy, not so different from all of you, too, I reckon. Listen ...' I said then, and I stood up—and I still can't believe I did all this, spoke that way to total strangers, acted so cool and so assured, because all the time, let me tell you, my heart was beating, it was going like bam, bam, bam as though those boys could hear it because, remember, this was seven something in the morning, in a quiet inner-city park, there was no one else around—and I started speaking then like it was all prepared. I told the boys about my life and about Jane Eyre and the writing classes and about my mother and father and how I missed them—and really, this is the heart of the short story, the reason Reed said I should write it in the first place, because I had a central 'incident' or 'pulse moment' as he calls it, the unexpected bit coming—bang—just like in *Jane Eyre* you might say, a certain thing happening that's like—whew!—this doesn't seem like real life, but it is. And I said then, 'Listen boys. Why don't you let me have this dog? I can see he's not yours. And you don't know what to do with him.'

'That's the truth,' one of them said.

'We didn't even want the fucking dog,' said another, right away, but looking at me as he spoke, and then saying, 'It wasn't my idea, you know.'

And then someone else said, 'Yeah, Keith. She's right. You didn't know what you were going to do with him. None of us did.'

Is how the conversation continued. And Keith, for he was the one who'd taken on Mr Rochester in the first place, told me he'd promised to look after a dog for someone who didn't want him but might be able to sell him on, but that if Keith took him off his hands, he could have the money, if there was any. They'd only got him the night before at the pub and someone there had said that the guy who had been interested wasn't even around. They had the choke chain, a bit of food in a bag, but no bowl, nothing really to feed him with … All this came out, bit by bit, as the boys started telling me their story, why, that same morning, after being up all night, roaming around with a dog they never really intended to have, it was a good thing I'd come upon them, walking out of the park from my morning run …

And, as for me, well, seeing some young men with a little dog, and leaving, after the conversation I had with them, with a pit bull terrier on a chain—one of the most dangerous dogs that exist, the papers say, with the most attacks of babies and toddlers, getting mauled in dog fights, you name it—it just shows how interesting life is, in stories and out of them. Because not only did I leave that morning with Mr Rochester on his little chain, but I'd told his previous 'owners', by the time I left, pretty much everything about myself and my own background, along with the full plot of *Jane Eyre*, and, though all four of them thought it sounded 'pretty fucking lame', they agreed that the scene in the red room had its merits. 'Yeah,' Steve said, quietly, as though to himself, after I'd finished telling that bit, 'my gran used to put me in a room like that.'

Anyhow, I've gone on and on, and Reed gave me, he gave all of us, a word limit and I need to start counting words now. But the reason I wanted to get it down as a story for class is because it was due to the events I've described that my life went into a change position when I came upon Mr Rochester that day. That was the 'incident', the 'pulse moment'—Reed said that to me straight away when I told him after class about what had happened to me in the park that morning and was asking whether it would be good for fiction. 'This is all a story, Katherine,' he said, 'a great story with a pulse moment that kicks the whole thing into life. You only have to get it onto the page,' and then we arranged to meet the next day and have a dog walk together because it turns out he was a pit bull man himself; he used to have one when he was a boy. 'Let's go for it,' he said, referring to the dog walk idea and doing that thing with his hair that I like so much, twisting it back with one hand so that he looks diffident—that's a great word—and shy.

So change, yes, change. Because now the same story is done and I'm still training, of course I'm still doing all that, but I'm writing more, too, and reading, and finding out more about words and language every day, and Mr Rochester is a total peach and we take him to the park, twice every day, Reed and I, and sometimes we meet up with the guys there—Steve and Keith and Dave and Kevin—and they take a look at Mr Rochester and I might tell them a bit more about his namesake because they occasionally ask after 'Jane' and what else went on in that book of hers and apparently, it's written all over me, Reed says, 'I could bring fiction to troubled kids in a new way.'

And Reed? You've probably guessed. Reed ... I married him. We decided that pretty soon after he said, 'Let's go for it,' about the dog walk but also meaning the idea of the two of us together. He said the whole thing lit up for him, as it did for me, the second I told him about my meeting with a so-called 'dangerous dog' and the boys who gave him to me and what we talked about that morning, the boys and I, and what happened then, and what happened next. After that, as he said, it was just a case of writing it down.

Flight Path

Helen said later that, like all horror stories, this one began with the smallest detail; a thing noticed that had seemed strange at the time—though you also might not have even noticed it: a small white feather on the road.

'That's from a snow goose, isn't it?' said Cal. He bent down to touch it, where the white edge of it, so delicate and bright, had attached itself to a chip of the tarmac. 'I've heard of these,' he said. 'My granny had a book all about geese, their habits, their seasons here … wow.'

We had all stopped. Cal knew stuff the rest of us could only listen to and learn from. His grandmother had lived here once, in this part of the North where we were, where we'd come to walk and be together. She had grown up here when there were still some villages and crofts left, when parts of the hills were still relatively empty and you could even swim in places, in some of the lochs and rivers. 'Sutherland used to be full of all kinds of birds,' Cal said now. 'Though I couldn't tell you for sure that that's where this came from. It could be a bit of stuffing, I guess, from an old cushion or something …' His voice trailed off as he let his fingertip smooth down the little bit of softness around the feather's spine. 'People used to stuff things with the plumage of birds. I've come across that, too, in books and films …'

'I heard there were swallows,' said Katherine. 'They used to come here every summer.'

'What's a swallow?' asked Jenny.

Helen turned. 'Jen!' She pretended to cuff her on the side of the head, laughed. 'I know you're joking, but you can't be *that* not interested!' Then she patted Jenny's arm, as though she were a little child. 'It's why we like it here, remember?' she said to her. 'So we can learn things? Get to know how it used to be?' She gestured around, the broken-up old tarmac road ahead of us, the hills on either side with their turbines like a forest of white columns stretching all the way to the horizon. 'Before they put all this on it, I mean. It's why we come here, isn't it? To try and … understand?'

For sure, that's what we always said was the reason for getting together three or four times a year to come north, to get to see this part of the country, think about the way it might have been. Though Jenny might have been doing it more for fitness, even she was into the excitement of those journeys of ours. How it felt like an act of terrorism, of clear and focused anti-social behaviour, it did, or rebellion, even, to be driving north to one of the power stations, leaving the car then and spending the next few days camping and walking across the hills.

'No, this is something …' Cal was still kneeling on the hot tarmac. It was so warm. The turbines around us, their white columns, seemed to shimmer in the bright light. None of the blades were turning. The day was calm and utterly quiet, extraordinary, actually, when there'd been such winds down south in Central Belt and we'd heard nothing but storm warnings coming from there in the days since we'd been away.

'Are you going to take it?' Helen asked. 'Like a souvenir?' The little feather fixed to the spot on the road looked bright and highly present, somehow, as though it were alive. A tiny object and yet now it was all we could see.

Cal just shook his head. 'I think we should leave it,' he said. 'Amazing though ...' He straightened up. 'I hope it is from a bird, I do hope so. That will be news to tell them.' He adjusted the weight he was carrying, tightened a strap. He had the largest pack, but he didn't mind that. It was the same on all our trips. He could manage the load because he was used to being out and walking; it was part of his PhD to be going over the country this way, tracking his own footprints. 'Psychogeography,' he called it, he said it had once been a kind of philosophy. We were all a bit in love with him, I suppose. We wanted to be near him, to do and listen to what he said and be changed by it. As David remarked once: 'He only needs to say the word. It could be any word.' And he was right, we'd learn it. Any place, to go there with him and walk with him, just to understand from him what it used to be like, how it might have seemed.

We'd only stopped because Cal had seen this thing the rest of us, I reckon, would have walked right past. He said there were so many species of birds here once, before the land was taken over by the power companies. And deer and rabbits and foxes, predators, all sorts. There'd been crofts with sheep and cows, and farms. And people, people living here then, and, yes, birds.

'I don't know much about flight patterns in detail, but I know that before all this became built over there were regular habits to animal and bird behaviour, according to weather,' he told us. By now, we'd headed up the side of a steep hill and were coming along the top. 'Animals on the move, birds on the move ... think about it,' Cal said. 'It must have been amazing.'

We were all of us paying attention, all quiet, imagining, trying to visualise what he was talking about, animals like deer and wild birds.

He had a way of expressing ideas and concepts that made you want to listen very carefully, stay near. I wished I could study with him. Write my own PhD about the North, about the days when it wasn't what it was like now. Be someone other than who I was, I suppose, is what I was really wishing for. A someone who might know what it was to plan and imagine and react and decide. A someone else who lived in a different way.

We carried on, one foot in front of another, following Cal's special pattern of walking and barely noticing how steep it was, while he told us about one particular flight path he'd read about that took in exactly—he stopped, looked at the old-fashioned kind of paper map he always brought with him—'Yes, here,' he said. 'I did read about this.' We'd all stopped. We realised the minute we did that we'd covered an enormous distance. In twenty minutes or so we'd come right up the side of that first hill and now the road had disappeared entirely, and we were nearly at the top. 'Look—' He had the section of the map out in front of us, entirely flat and unruffled. Even up on the summit of the hill, the air was shock still, like glass. Each turbine was motionless. 'It's a flight that takes in this part of the country exactly,' Cal was saying. 'Between these two points—' he showed Helen and Katherine the places on the map. 'And, yes, the book. I remember it was a story and wild geese were in the title, I remember that, and it was about how people used to be, living with the land around them, and their communities. I wish I could tell you who it was by …'

He went quiet then; he might have been thinking about his family, his parents who never came up here at all even though when his mother was a girl, she had spent every holiday with her mother in the old house before it had had to be fully abandoned. 'There'd been a joke back in those days,' he'd told us once, 'when people still used to come to visit up here, tourists, from all over the world. They'd drive up from the south and had been told if they wanted directions, they need only remember the old saying, "I know we can't be there yet because I can still see the hills." Ha ha.' He said that down south they used to call the country up here 'Monstrous North'. For what people had let happen to the land.

He looked up and around him at the white turbine columns that were everywhere, all around us, and as far as we could see. 'Can you believe what it must have been like once, though?'

'Empty?' said Jenny.

'Beautiful,' said Helen.

'That was what the book was about,' Cal said. 'Beauty.'

The day was moving on, we'd been walking since early morning and not thinking much about the time, but now, with the mighty stillness of thought upon us, and the clear bright peculiarity of the day—so very quiet as to have something wrong with it, almost, when there was supposed to be such wind elsewhere—time seemed held, arrested. It must have been about noon, but hard to tell in that endless strange sunlight cast all around us. We were tired from the steep climb, but also not tired. These walks of Cal's were not easy, but we never minded the difficulty of an ascent, or weather; he kept everyone motivated that way. He had a leader's method and moved us on with his talks of the past and ideas of other ways of living. Geography as psychic, as emotional. The idea of just being in a place like this, outside, open to anything that might happen and not knowing when you might go back to the Belt. Or that you might never return there. You might just keep walking.

Katherine would often say she had the feeling he was using us, old friends after all, as a sort of test. How much could he ask of us to do with him, that we would do it? How far for him would we go?

We started up again, along the tops towards the north side of a set of low hills in the distance that gave way to a range behind, blue and lovely, though you could make out the spikes of white along the horizon line. Cal had said that if we could get to that point below the line, there was an old electrics hut he knew about that we could stay in. I kept thinking about that feather, back there on the road. Its clear spine, the gentle movement of it as Cal had touched it with the tip of his finger. *Look at that* ... As we went on, walking along the high ridge through the forest of white columns, and with each step getting higher and higher as though rising above ourselves, above even the great structures that were all around us—as though they didn't matter and we could be free. As though we might even be part of that other world, I suppose, is how we felt, looking back on it. That other landscape of the past. And who might we be in it? What might our life be like then? A sort of dream?

With all that we'd been talking about, thinking about, about the way things had been once, the loveliness of it, the emptiness, nothing could have prepared us for what was to happen next. Helen dropped to her knees—'I can't breathe,' she said, then, 'Oh my God!'—and we were all looking up together—and who could have imagined it? Or known, from its appearance, how it would be? But there, coming out of the sky behind us, a great mass was approaching. In a split second it was practically overhead and we could see it, the approach of birds. Hundreds and hundreds of real flying birds, actual birds with wings that moved, and beaks and claws, coming through the turbines and fitting between them in one great perfect shape of flight, utterly unimpeded, unaffected by anything other than the huge massed might of their own forward motion .... We'd had a moment to take it in, that they were coming straight towards us, then we were surrounded by them, caught up entirely in the onward rush of their bodies and feathers and flight, the flapping of their flying, and their wild, wild cries.

We'd thought we were going to die. It was impossible to breathe, the sense of that almighty motion, of force of will and movement and onward propulsion, all around us, stifling us, and the beat of wings behind and above us, around us and in front of us … an endless flight, it seemed, of these living things, these actual flocks of birds that were in front and below and behind so the air was no longer air but only beaks and claws and wings and heads and feathers and bodies of birds as though there was nothing else to exist in the world, as though there could be nothing else, no person, no turbine, no piece of ground nor space of sky, but only this rush of terror and horror and wonder and beauty, and heaven and hell …

And then they were gone. The sound, deafening a second ago, was already getting fainter, and the air was clearing; the great dark shadow of their presence had already been swept away and was dissolved into distance. It was light again. We were all of us on the ground, coughing, spluttering, hardly able to see. What was that, that had happened? Was it real? They'd been birds we'd seen, alive and flying, real birds, and we'd been part of them as though we were going to be caught up by them and hurled on with them, suffocated, surrounded by them, by their sharp beaks and claws … Though we realised, too, as soon as we recovered, that apart from Cal, none of us had actually felt so much as the touch of a single feather. Not a graze, not a scratch. We were all absolutely unharmed.

Only, as Helen said, this was a horror story, remember? And an announcement had been made, the annunciation of a white feather on the road. Had it really been only that morning when we had seen it? When Cal had bent to put the tip of his finger to its fragile edge? A feather, we'd all thought then. Who would have believed it?

Nothing made any sense, and yet everything did.

For yes, only Cal had been marked by what had happened—a thin, thin line of blood like the tracery of a single claw that ran down the length of his bare arm and fanned out along his fingers. 'Just then,' he said, 'what happened to us …' His words were quiet in the silence that followed the birds' departure. 'We were part of their migration.' His eyes were trained on distance, looking to where the birds had gone, to the horizon that had taken them in. It may have been that he thought he was talking to us, but really he was only speaking to himself. 'Think about it …' he said.

Nothing else was apparent. Nothing else had seemed to alter. The air was empty. The sky, just as blue and bright, and everything was still. Only the blades started turning then, slowly at first, in the slightest suggestion of a light breeze, and then in a gust of wind beginning fully their rotations. *Part of their migration …* And Cal was walking away.

David called after him. 'Ah, man. C'mon. *Migration?* What kind of a word is that?' We all of us started talking then—'What's going on? What's happening?' Behaving as though Cal was still part of our conversation, as though he was with us, as though nothing had changed. Because what was that he'd said? 'Migration?' Katherine asked. 'Is that what you said?' 'Cal?' 'Cal?' But I think we'd all known, from the minute we'd seen that thin run of blood down his arm, that he was lost to us.

'What are you doing?' David started running after him. The wind was picking up, getting stronger. 'What did you say?' he was shouting out to Cal. 'What kind of a word?' But Cal was far enough away that he would have never been able to hear. He was already up off the side of the next hill and was walking along the top of it and then over, walking quickly, despite the wind, the changing weather, and we were all running by then, trying to catch up with him, shouting,

'Cal!' Calling to him, wanting him to come back to us and running as though we would be able to catch up with him when he was already so far away and the wind so strong by then we couldn't run against it—while he was only walking on as though through it, with it, as though the wind was carrying him.

The white blades were turning faster now, and faster, as though awakened from a sleep, picking up speed and strength and whirring into life. If this was a horror story, it was a horror story only for us. The wind ricocheting across the hills, gale forces coming full at us, as still we called 'Cal!' 'Come on!' 'Please!'—as though he might hear us when he was walking so clearly, so cleanly away that he may as well have been in another world.

Even so, we tried to reach him, still trying, calling, in a wind so strong that in the end it was too much for us to try to follow him, to go after him, with the force of the gales only pushing us back and the turbine arms spinning at such a rate that the sound of them was terrible. And we had to turn away from him then. We ran. Back down the side of the hill and down, the wind at our backs to push us on, falling and tumbling to get back and down, down to where we'd come from, down all the way to the road, and from there to the car … Running away while all the time Cal walked on into the distance, further and further gone into the place where the birds were, where he could hear their wild and lovely cries … As one by one around us the turbine blades caught fire and the air began to burn.

King Country

Their father had always let them handle the guns so they thought nothing of allowing me to touch them. Though their father was not someone I could ever speak to or know. He was a frightening man with 'a little war wound' he called it, a long red scar from where a stallion had bitten him on the thigh right through to the bone, and it made him suck his breath in between his teeth and whisper 'Christ' when he had to do something in a hurry—get up, say, to give one of his boys a whack if they'd been causing trouble, or bend over to pick up a heavy bag or sack off the ground. 'Christ Jesus' sometimes, he'd say then, when the wound perhaps hurt him, the s's in the words sounding through those strong white teeth in his dark, tanned face. I was a child but I desired him then, before I knew what desire was. 'To come in' was the phrase I used, privately, to myself. To know what it was to be entirely in love.

But you can't be in love with your best friends' father—I knew that too, and the Carter boys were my best friends. Not only Taylor, who was in my class at school and the skinniest, but Kip and Tommy, who were both older but let me be in their gang, and they were all three of them 'mean buggers' their father called them. 'Come here, you lot!' he'd shout when he got back to the house after a big day out in the bush where he was working. 'Get inside', and he'd whistle them in like they were a pack of dogs and it made them yell with pleasure when he did it. 'Ah, yah Pappy!' they'd scream back at him, charging around the place, tackling him, and running away just as fast. They were acting like they were terrified only they were excited, excited by his presence, and by the things they'd done while he'd been away. 'We'll have your guts,' Kip said to me once, when making me promise on some secret or other—a cat killed or some boy at school Tommy had cut—that I'd never tell. 'God's truth' all three of them reminded me. 'We'll hurt you if you squeal.'

Their father knew the boys were tough but the exact nature of their secrets was kept from him—and they were many. Kip, who was thirteen and like a man, led on all the games and had a million cruel actions he could generate, like a machine, and then want to hide from. Like he'd skinned a rabbit when it was still half alive and spat muck in the face of a girl we met once at the gas station because she was pretty, after he'd got her behind one of the old disused pumps and put his hand up her dress. He'd already used sticks for sex, he said, and knew exactly what he was doing. Taylor told me he'd done it loads, and what did the rest of us know about it, anyhow? I couldn't think but didn't dare ask in case Kip realised I might be a girl myself and would use one of those sticks on me. He did other things, yes, but I didn't mind because I wasn't really a girl. With the Carters I could be who I wanted and stay that way; they would let me be a boy with them. So I might learn from them how to cut up animals and sell their fur, build forts from willow and fish for eels with a nail in the same way they'd taught me how to swear and run fast across rocks in bare feet and dive off the cliff straight down into the water. Of course I could come near guns and traps and knives and not be frightened. Everything was there before me, is how it seemed. A life laid out. As though all through the time of knowing that family I could be someone who was not a stupid girl but just wear shorts and have my shirt off, free out there in the sun and wind with them, and sometimes my skin peeled off so underneath the new pink layer showed up, but I didn't mind. 'You're tough, alright,' Kip told me when we were kissing. 'You'll do.'

There was a mother in the picture but we didn't talk about her much. I never knew her name and the boys only called her 'Ma', which was all wrong for someone who held her body in the world the way she did, who took her time. It was only when I grew up myself and saw women who had that same look of quiet confidence, like an animal in the sunshine just sitting there like it's never planning to move, that I realised what beauty was: the bare minimum of a thing to create the largest, largest effect. I saw women like Mrs Carter then, much later in my life when there were women, and more women ... But back in those days I didn't have the vocabulary to describe someone who knew exactly what they could do with the wild and generous terms granted by their own body. She was there in the background, maybe, but with an aliveness running all the way through her, and her boys seemed to feel it too, putting their hands on her as if to take some charge off her, 'Ahhhh, Ma. Go on. Go *on*.' I think about that now, the memory of her stance, her immobility while they crowded around. I can't remember anything she would say or do in response—while her husband, by contrast, seemed to surge and spark with words and activity. It was as though he was fired up, so charged by those rifles of his kept on a table in the back room, the boxes of bullets and knives beside, that he might use them any second and the whole house would explode. 'Those are things I need for work!' he would yell at the boys. 'Don't you lot move stuff when you go in there. I don't mind you having a play, you need to learn how to manage a gun. But none of it's for your use. Not now!' 'But when, Pappy?' the boys would shout back at him because, of course, we did go in, and the boys handled the guns all the time.

'When?' And Mr Carter would raise his arm as if he was going to give Kip a whipping but he'd be grinning, laughing, kind of. 'When I decide!' he'd yell back. 'That's bloody when!' looking at me, too, with his black eyes. 'And you,' he said. 'Don't think you're not part of this. You can touch, you know full well, but you can't use.'

No wonder his sons never told him, they never would dare, of what they got up to, whether they had access to their father's guns or not—of the animals Kip shot with his own BB rifle, though it was only supposed to be for rabbits, or the things Tommy and Taylor did to the other kids at school. Their father had rules. You could be tough but not disobedient, wild but not cruel. And for sure all three made certain I'd never give away some fact that might show how far they'd transgressed—that I'd seen Taylor put a rat on the teacher's desk, say, still moving but its guts all out, and that he swore and shouted most of the time through lessons. James Carter was not to know about any of it. Those rules of his were deep in his boys even while they disobeyed them, over and over again and all the time terrified of what he'd do to them if he found out. It was why they liked to keep reminding me, they said, of ammunition and triggers and of safety catches that could be released. 'Don't be frightened, scared-y. But know what this is,' Tommy waved his father's oldest rifle around, pointing it at my heart. 'Boom. Get it? Be careful. You better be.'

For my part though, they need never have worried that I would tell. Even with the blood banging in my head for fear, standing there with them while Kip broke open the rifles one by one and cleaned inside with an oily rag, kidding me on that there were bullets in the chamber while he did it. I wanted, more than any feeling normally would have allowed, to belong to all three of those boys forever and to that father of theirs. And so I did touch the guns. I picked them up, put them down. In order to be that 'you as well' as Mr Carter had looked at me and said. To be a brother, a son. A something else I couldn't explain that had nothing to do with my life at my own house with my own parents, that would let me scream around the place and be grabbed and brought to the ground. To be able to put my arms around a waist like Mr Carter put his arms around his wife's body—as though she was a beautiful wild animal, only he had caught her. To be similarly enclosed. To be ... *Come in.* This was what kept me going back to the Carters, holding my tongue. Their house only down the road, but another world.

They'd lost everything, I found out later, because Mr Carter had been in prison somewhere up north for hurting a man and people couldn't see past it to give him any kind of proper job. For these reasons he'd had to make do 'on the side' as he called it, rogue farming a few acres that he'd dug himself out of the bush forty miles or so away from town. That, and a bit of culling for the forestry commission and managing some timber work for them, kept him going, you might say. But what does it mean, really, 'kept him going'? I think about that now. When it was the kind of country that closed up behind you as fast as you went in, and with any track grown over just as quickly as it had been made? So James Carter could do that, manage being there on his own, because, my father told me once, he didn't have a choice and he was courageous, 'virtuous', the word my father used. 'He is someone with great will,' my father said, 'and it's a virtuous will'—though he didn't want me hanging around the Carters even so. Most people knew about them—as my father did, and my mother, and kids at school knew and whispered about it ... About what Mr Carter had done. 'But,' my father said, 'that man wouldn't have been the first to have had some bad luck and to want to make do for income with a bit of cleared land.' There would always be a kind of person who sat outside the life led in that part of the country, in those days. My parents seemed to have an understanding about it. Even so, we'd only recently moved to that town and my father had a job with a clean, tidy car to take him to work each day, not a big old dirty truck that didn't always start, and in the end, for all his talk, he would have wished me, as my mother did, to be more like other girls, think about different things.

But my mind was full up with Mr Carter and his boys. From the day I first saw them I couldn't take my eyes off them; the way they dressed, the way they spoke. They didn't seem to care about anyone. So when Taylor said, 'Come on', when I went up to him at the end of my first week at the new school to look at his bike which he told me he'd stolen and then let me ride bareback home with him to his house … it was like a hook. Something grabbing at me, pulling me along, and it wasn't going to be possible afterwards for me to think about anything else. The Carters didn't have a garden with little flowers and the front door always closed. Their place went straight onto paddock and had a broken-down verandah round the back you could live out on if you wanted, Taylor told me that first day. From there, even at night, he said, you could see all the way off to the foothills of where his father went on his own for work. He pointed it out, the dark mass of land in the distance. Urewera, Taylor said. King Country. The whole area was. All three boys talking about it as though it was a place that existed only in the future, like a fairy tale or fable or history, where you could never arrive at, only want to go.

Which is how we imagined it, all the time. How dangerous it would be there, to be inside that land. Somewhere with seasons and days not seeming to apply, it was that dark down in the valleys, with rivers running at spate and all sluiced up with mud and scree. There were sharp hard precipices, the boys told me, and cliffs dropping down to the bush floor where giant trees grew, their tops blocking out the sun like a black roof above your head. We'd be all four of us out on that verandah, talking about it, thinking about it. And what it would be like to be one man on his own in such a place and the choices he would have to make, the exact preparations he would need to consider in order to be safe … Of course he would have to have the guns in there with him. Because it was his job, the boys told me—to herd and cull and trap and shoot and cut up for sale and cut down. There were dangerous wild pigs and boar in those mountains, Taylor showed off about in school. Mr Carter had given him a tusk as a memento, like a giant's yellow tooth with a pointed tip that could ram through anything—and where his father went there were hundreds of these kinds of animals, Taylor told the kids in class, horses, great herds of deer, goats. There were possum traps filled with poisoned creatures that his father needed to clear, nets and dams busting out with conger eels that behaved like sharks and were thick as a man's arm. 'Be quiet, Taylor Carter,' our teacher would say, 'we all know about your father.' But Taylor wouldn't be quiet. It really was King Country, he said, with a King's Ransom in there and nothing you couldn't shoot, snare and butcher. And it was being paid to you, see? Like it was given. 'Meat or money?' That's what Mr Carter shouted out to us, when he got back from one of his trips, after being away for two weeks or more, and it meant he had money from the Government and something on the back of the truck that we could eat. So Taylor was right. Here was everything we needed, everything. And for sure, you could think about that as you sat on the Carter's back verandah, smoking cigarette ends and eating jam sandwiches and looking out onto the piece of land one man had come home from, arrived standing in the doorway as tall as the ceiling with his pack and his dogs and the truck outside still hot and covered with mud. Meat or money, alright. And all because of him.

Remembering this, those trips and how they were presented, the way the boys talked about them, describing everything down to the smallest detail … Of course I can see now that they understood what their father was doing to make a living in a way I never could have. But they were gracious, I think, in not letting on; instead making me feel that all four of us together could only imagine the way it was for him. Because, really, how could I expect to share their understanding, have anything of their lives—though that first day of going home with Taylor turned into weeks and months that I thought would last forever. All through the spring and summer I lived so close to that family you'd think I might have seen more, be told more, shown more. But, in the end, despite the tense animal feeling of the boys' father pressing on me exactly an image of who, when I grew up, I wanted to be, and for all the rich feeling come from his wife and sons to include me in their lives, I never knew that much about the Carters. They were on their own. And, glamorous as they were to me, I was aware even then that being alone was probably how it had always been for them. A condition fixed in and deep. Something they carried. But what do you do with narrative like this? Gather it up? Even call it a story? For sure, I can write, despite—or maybe because of—their isolation, the Carters seemed to belong to that part of the North Island in a way others I've met since who were born around there don't. And though I know the area James Carter farmed and worked doesn't necessarily form the shape of something I can use for fiction—it's too real for that—even so, to think of how a part of the land stood in relation to the rest of us, so far away it seems from our small towns and cities, far from everything, does remind me of parables, myths. It's there on the page before me—a shadowed region on the map—as though it marks out a memory that has never gone away. 'Te Urewera. King Country.' Just to say the words made me feel like a man.

Myths don't come out of speaking, though. It's been a long time since a story would arrive that way out of the dark. You need light to reveal what's happening, and written explanation, light's words and understanding. Without exposure any act or deed remains as mute and invisible as any of the boys' pitiless unspoken games. So it was that Mr Carter, who for so long had seemed to be someone in a certain kind of narrative, terrifying and mesmerising in the things he did, snaking his arm around his wife or pulling his youngest son up onto his shoulder and biting his bare leg, putting Kip and Tommy to the ground so that he could keep them down there and then kiss them ... Was also, in another kind of account, someone else altogether. And while he'd been busy being the one I watched and wanted, that presence in a room, that body, with those words and that mouth and his eyes and his breathing, right there beside me, he had also been another man, a stranger, you might say, who I didn't see until he was demonstrated to me, as he was in the end, in full sunlight, in the middle of a bright morning.

That wasn't until the very end of summer, though, when I found out about the other version. It begins just before we were due to go back to school and the boys told me their father had come home from one of his early autumn trips, as he called them, and had decided that he was going to take us out with him. That was when, exactly, a shift occurred in the pattern of how things up until then had been. Because a trip with him now? After all this time? We couldn't believe it. It simply made no sense.

But we didn't want to ask too many questions, either. For to be going, just to know that this time when he left the house Mr Carter wouldn't be alone but that we'd be there with him, gone into the mysterious place that had been the destination of our thoughts and stories ... it was a gift. As though a mighty, mighty gift. We'd be leaving very early in the morning, he said, working all day and not getting back until late at night. He took us into the room with the guns to tell us. That he was bringing us with him to the farm he'd made, he said, because there were things to be sorted out there, and in a hurry. That we'd need protective clothes. Wet weather gear for where the river was dammed, reinforced boots. He made us remember it as a list. Tarpaulins. Petrol. The guns, of course we'd be taking the guns, and knives and sacks and kerosene. It was extraordinary even to hear him say the words 'leaving', 'working', 'getting back late at night'—with us there in his plans alongside them. It was the rag end of the holidays and we'd long ago given up thinking anything more was going to happen with that season. The paddocks were chewed down and dry and we'd had a lifetime, it seemed, Kip and Tommy and Taylor and I, of being on our own and wishing we could go with Mr Carter every time he left but instead only watching him load up the dogs and his pack and drive away. So, really, yes. It was like a gift. That after all those days and weeks … this time he wouldn't be alone because we'd be part of it, what he was doing, and adding to it—to help with getting the vegetables in, he said, because the goats had got out and been at them and we'd need to move fast or there'd be nothing left, nor in the traps or in the dam. 'I don't want you with me,' he'd told Tommy. 'But I need you. I need—' and here my heart could barely contain its jump '—all four of you boys.' And why hadn't he asked us earlier? Tommy didn't know, no one knew. And how could it be that James Carter would ever need anybody? When there was nothing he couldn't manage himself, no action large or small he couldn't have got on with himself in his own way like he always did? That 'I need you' like an echo that wasn't sounding true.

Now, of course, writing all this through, one story into another, I can understand in the way the child never could that the reason all this was happening was only that his time had come. His taking a bunch of kids with him that day a way of making a final plea, I suppose, an attempt to speak back to and counter actions already taken against him over, what, months? More than. Before the year had started, most probably. For more than a year. Before I even moved to that town and came to know the Carters—though my presence there among them hadn't helped any, I found out later. Even so, it had taken all those days and weeks and months until that particular week, the end of the summer holidays and the vegetables not nearly half ready by then, for his life, for the things James Carter had managed to do in order to gain a living from his life, in that place, at that time, to become at last impossible for him. Kip said his father had told him that once we were there, right inside the country, he would be allowed to use his 44 on any animals we came across that played up; that Tommy could take the BB as well, 'just in case'. But just in case, what? I remember that thought formed an entire shape in my mind. Mr Carter had hurt a man up north, I knew; and there'd been a gun involved then. Something below the words carrying more menace than any images of animal wildness or the uncertainty of terrain ... 'Shoot any mean-looking bugger on four legs that even looks at you,' Kip said his father had told him. He was beside himself with power. 'Pappy doesn't know how much skill I have in all that,' he said. 'And don't you say a word about any of it, either.' We were around the side of the house where there were no windows so we couldn't be seen. The peel on my skin had healed over and you couldn't even tell I'd been burnt. 'Watch me when I'm in there,' he whispered, his breath hot at my ear. 'I'm going to know exactly what to do.'

The fact, as I can only imagine it, is that James Carter had brought us with him that day—children, after all—in order that it might shame them, somehow ... Those men who were waiting for him in the road that day. That our presence might have said to them:

Look. I am the same as you. I have a family. A life. Not so different, don't you see? As though the opinions and criticisms that had taken shape and formed before I even met Taylor the first day at my new school and had amassed might still be dissolved, for those men to see children there with him … That there might be a chance of saving things here, the land, the livelihood, that life. But no. The chatter and gossip had so long been turned into persuasion against the dangerous father who'd come down from some prison up north that it could only further harden with our presence. For when we arrived at the entrance to the track that had been cut into the side of the road, that would lead into the farmed area made out of nothing, out of nowhere, there they were. A roadblock of sorts. Half a dozen armed men. And Kip the one who picked up the 44 and used it.

'Like father like son,' the men had jeered when the air had settled. 'No going back now, laddie. It's all over for you here.'

For what had he expected? That the outcome could be any different? Who did he think he was? That he might be somehow immune? Just as he'd thought he could come here in the first place and live here in a respectable community along with everyone else? That that was what attempted murder left you with? That you could just ignore the past? And the next thing you know the new family who've moved down the road would take up with them? Like that silly tomboy daughter who had thought she could do that? Just let herself, what? '*Come in* …'? What then, eh? People would have said. That others might start doing the same? So the talk had gone on. Decisions made that something had better be done and there were men who would do it. Because who did James Carter think he was? As one of them said to him that morning in the road, before Kip even fired the shot, coming forward and poking him in the chest with his long ugly finger. 'Who do you think you are, laddie? Eh? Who?'

Is how it all played out that morning in bright sunshine, in the light. And that one individual against the rest could have really believed any gesture he might make would stop the talk, their actions, have them think again … I shall never know the reality and circumstances of such detail and mind. Only that what I saw that morning must have been just another in a whole series of incidents and insults that I hadn't witnessed; gestures and speeches played out in other places far from the edge of the dirt track that provided our theatre for the day. When it became the case, on this one morning, just before school went back, that a series of interventions already taken place, carried out by a group of just a few, maybe, but with the weight of prejudice and judgement behind them, would become impossible for one man to bear. That prison sentence, something he could never escape, never—so it would only ever be just a matter of time before an itinerant family would be driven out from a town by those who felt they'd been there long enough.

I have put myself in this story as though I am part of it, as though I might ask questions and describe and try and understand—but answers don't exist for any of it. What is left for me instead is the sure knowledge I have now, that the girl in the story could never have possessed, that by the time Mr Carter called us into the room with the guns to tell us we were going into the bush with him it was already too late. The time had passed long ago before bringing a truck full of kids with him might have made a difference to men's minds made up. They were ready and waiting for him by the time we arrived in sight of the dirt track. We turned the corner, and there they were.

And how I remember it all, in sharp, sharp detail. How Mr Carter stopped the truck. How for the first few seconds nothing happened. There were, I would say, six or maybe more men, maybe eight, all holding rifles. They just stood there. We hadn't stopped in a hurry, Mr Carter hadn't slammed on the brakes; he'd just slowly drawn the truck down to a halt, and then we sat, we waited. The men shuffled a little as they arranged themselves, they wanted us to see what they were carrying. It was a bright, bright late summer morning. The wind had disappeared, everything was still. Through the rear window of the truck, I could see Mr Carter in the cab, the back of his dark head in the sunshine, his brown hands on the steering wheel. I remember how I wanted to reach through the glass and touch his head, his hair, the back of his neck, and his hands, to lay my own hand upon his. All the gear was on the back of the truck but he had his own rifle, I could see that, too, through the window of the cab. It was laid out on the seat beside him as though it were something that was also watching, waiting. Seconds continued to pass, one second, another second … then he took his hands off the wheel, opened the cab door and got out. He walked towards the group of men where they were standing hard up next to each other, looking at him. He'd left the rifle where it was, laid down on the seat of the cab.

I don't think I knew or had seen any of those men before, and I only found out later that they were the same group who'd been following someone they'd targeted as an outsider from as early as late winter. They'd been checking up on him, what he had been doing, and then going in after and interfering, maiming his stock when he'd thought at first it was wild pigs doing that, weakening his fence posts that he wouldn't notice at first maybe but then a part of his enclosure line wouldn't hold, and he'd have to do it all over. Bit by bit, in this way, they had acted against him. One thing, another thing. And of course he had never said. Well, the boys never said anything about it to me, I suppose is what I am really saying. Because in their house it wasn't the kind of thing anyone would talk about in front of me, that the Carters were starting to realise people might be acting on their talk because they just couldn't let go of the past; people like that couldn't. And who knows? One of those men standing there to block our way that morning might have been a brother to the man who'd been hurt up north all that time ago. Or maybe there was someone who knew someone who knew. There could be any number of reasons people might have had, that he would have kept to himself, James Carter would have, and tried to keep, too, from his boys; reasons that would have made those men feel justified in damaging the work that he had established, the paddocks created out of undergrowth, the vegetable plots and the traps he'd laid and dams made for fishing and drainage, fresh plantings of fruit trees and saplings.

People were never going to leave him alone. They weren't going to understand or forgive what he'd done in the past, the kind of family they were—and now here these men were with their weapons to prove it. And that must have been a hard enough scene to play, for sure, in that morning's grim theatre. To have to get out of the truck and face those men with their stupid guns … walk up to them as he walked up to them, as though to reason with them, as though he might have tried … we watched the whole thing, his boys watched, in the yellow light of day, and saw that all of this had been allowed, that Mr Carter himself had allowed it. Those grown men taunting him as though he were the child, calling him and his family out as criminals, as thugs and as murderers and thieves … we had to see it all, hear it all. That if it came to it, they said, firearms would be used, well then, they'd have a reason, they said, 'Oh, we'd have a reason, alright.' One of them finally lifting up his rifle and aiming it. 'C'mon laddie, let's see what you're made of. You with that woman of yours and your kids no more than animals. Who do you think you are?'

So I watched him stand his ground. His boys watched, the four of us up on the back of the truck, we could see everything from there—and he never went back for his gun. He'd just left it in the cab where it had been laid out beside him like a live thing that could jump only he wasn't allowing it, standing so quietly there in the road, taking what those men were saying to him, and taking it, the engine of the truck still running, the door of the cab open … It was as though he had thought he might just step out to deal with the situation, the men and then get back into the truck again as easy, be on his way. But without anyone noticing, Kip had got off the back and was round the side, had grabbed the rifle and aimed and fired.

The shot rang out. For a fraction of a second there was nothing but that, the shot, the ring of it. And then a million birds were flung upwards into the sky and the sky went black with the sound of their screaming. Kip had aimed at the centre of the group of men, I saw him, but he had lifted the rifle and it was sky that took the blow. Nothing else had been intended. And yet … that word. Intended. Whoever cares what has been intended? The shot had sounded—and whether it's a boy's bullet meant for air, or a man's that is for a leg or for a foot, which, as I found out years later, was where his father's bullet once, long ago and to his shame, had been intended … still, it makes no difference what's intended. The shot rang out now, as then, with all its dark consequences risen up behind it. The shot, the gun. The stupid, stupid gun. His father turned, saw Kip, the weapon in his hands. 'Ah, Christ,' he said. 'My boy. What have you done?'

Kip dropped the rifle then. He turned to his father, his father shook his head. As though to say, 'No …' As though in a voice I'd never heard before, vastly changed. And Kip started shouting, shouting something to his father, to the men—idiot words, crazy words. I could hear him, see him, standing there gesturing and yelling, Tommy and Taylor and I could see … Though his father had him by the arms now, and was holding him in so he couldn't move, saying something to him in a voice that must have been as loud as his son's but was somehow as very, very quiet as that 'No … No …' Still Kip was shouting and not stopping, twisting and yelling, going on and on, these crazy words … this oldest son. This grown-up boy, more a young man than a boy, shouting as though he would never stop, only shouting, going on and on—but then his father said something else to him, whispered in his ear, and Kip became quiet then. He let himself be held. Another second or two passed, and the two of them turned; the son released from his father's arms, his face ruined with tears and with rage and shame, and the two of them walked back to the truck and got inside. One of the men kicked a dog then and killed it. All the dogs had leapt off the truck the minute they'd sensed danger and they'd been on the road, barking and snarling, though Mr Carter had kept on at them to get inside. Still their instincts to protect ran high and they would only stay near him, circling around him, ready to move into attack the second they needed to, their teeth bared, curling and weaving, their bodies low to the ground … And yes, the little black and white collie that got too close to one of the men received a blow to the head with the butt of a rifle and with a yelp fell down, convulsing. Two or three more boots to its head followed, and to its belly, and then it was kicked in a heap to the side of the road. Still Mr Carter didn't do anything. It was one of his sheepdogs, the collie, not a pig dog who would not have taken a kick so easy, and he waited a minute, acknowledging what had happened, then whistled the rest of them in and they rushed to him, leaping up onto the back of the truck as he turned on the ignition and reversed, edging into the ditch so he could turn, manoeuvre the truck around and we could go back the same way we came. I could hear the men yelling, 'She's not one of your bloody gang. She's just a girl and you lot have no business with our people. Get out and go back to where you came from.' Their voices should have been silenced by the sound of the engine's revs but they were not. 'Ya bloody coward,' I heard. 'What are you doing here, thinking you can live here with the rest of us? Get out!' I could still hear them, with the road emptying behind us and the dog's black and white body, streaked with red, getting smaller and smaller, as we drove away.

That's what light gives. Seeing. And no wonder those boys of long ago wanted to keep everything in the dark. You might say the writer would come in at this point, to remark on that, on the seen and the unseen—the stick and poke of detail like the patterning of Kip's school ink tattoos … I could spend pages bringing certain parts of the story out: Look at this here, and here and here—but what then? It's not where any of this was ever leading. Nor what happened to me afterwards, the decisions about my own life I went on to make, when this account is finished and done with and I'd had to leave the Carters behind me, put on a dress and become a girl. Because all the kinds of secrets we children kept that seemed once upon a time to scream so loud, the skinning and killing and the going after small animals still live in Kip's traps when we got to them … That squealing and violence, that terror … come to be as nothing next to the knowledge spread out on that bright day—of who James Carter was, who he had become, who he'd had to be. He didn't say anything to us after we got back to the house, and we left all the gear we'd taken with us just sitting on the back of the truck like anyone might take it, and maybe they did. And he didn't say anything either, to Kip, about his use of the gun, or about the little dog that had been killed. And he didn't say anything about the words we'd heard, what those men had said, the things they'd done.

All of it became history, disappeared into time—in the same way years later when I came back to that part of the country where I'd grown up to try and find out something about the Carters then, I couldn't. Who they were, where they might have gone, where they'd come from, maybe, that records might have been kept ... For there were none of course. They'd arrived and left again, as people like them do. Arriving and leaving. Leaving, always leaving, because people like them can never stay. They get lost, don't they, through the years? And the writer can't find them again when she goes to the place where they'd lived, the house more broken up than ever when I saw it again and the family who are there now, they've never heard of the Carters or an old crime or of land that was once farmed forty miles out of town somewhere in the foothills of the Ureweras because it's all sealed up again, that story, with fresh growth, trees even. The mud so rich and red it can't help but run back to make things the way they have always been, and even if I wanted to, I couldn't find the opening into land one man once made.

He'd been imprisoned for shooting at someone who had been with a young woman out the back of one of those wild pubs they have up north and was mistreating her, that's what I did know. It was the kind of place with no closing hours, no rules at all, and he had seen her, the woman who would become his wife, being forced up against a wall and held by the throat, and he had acted. That was what people also talked about, whispered about. It was laughter as well as fear that kept the Carters away from the rest. Because she was to become his own wife. Drink spoke, and because it was a place shearing gangs knew about and came to, and people from all over the country, in logging companies or with the vermin outfits, deer and possum culling. They would have asked what was she doing there in the first place, a woman on her own like that. When anyone knew anything could go on in those hot dark nights with the fluorescent strip light turned up inside and the smoke of drinking and men's talk ... So what did she expect? Alone—and all eyes on her because she was something, she was, and with the man she would marry having eyes for her in the same way after all. So when some trapper had his hands on her, took her from behind and held her there against the wall where he thought no one could see, Jim Carter just went out and picked the rifle off the passenger seat in his ute—someone told me all this years later who had been there, who had seen. The other had his pants open when Carter got there, he said, round the side of the building in the dark where his wife wasn't even crying out, she'd gone so still she was like a branch.

'My spirit,' Kip used to tell me, 'comes from my Pappy's own bad man blood. What he's made of,' he used to say, 'I've got inside me. See?'

But the story doesn't go like that, does it? As though it were another of the boys' dumb games? Just another stupid story of another stupid gun? Nor is it finished by going back to pick up the lost and also remembered details out of the dark. Because none of that information—Kip's rifle going off, and his father's before him, all those years ago that he would spend all his life regretting—is what I am left with here. In fact, by now there are no dumb rifles left in this story at all. There's no terror. There's no 'Boom'. It's all quiet here. It finishes with the weapons gone dead.

I'd run inside the house like Taylor told me, to get matches so we could smoke out back and stay that night on the verandah. That after everything that had gone on that day, the boys might leave their father alone, and their mother, and so I would be the one who would go into the house to get a light. And there are no sentences or phrases—nothing that comes close to the terrible softness that was present in the room that night and more frightening to me than any of the boys' actions, or anything that went on in their father's world—for the still quietness of what I saw, his head down upon her shoulder, and her low words as she stroked his head … 'It's okay …

It's okay ...' I took the matches, they didn't see me, and I ran back outside to where the boys were waiting.

In the end, then, you might say, though I've failed to find the words, I did finally learn, on my last night spent with them, something of what it was to be part of that family after all, in those few seconds, to learn it. To be '*come in*' at last to the quietness of what was being brought about indoors, enacted there, which those boys would have known about, of course, and seen, no doubt many, many times before ... Still, I find myself standing back from what I have effected, after all. Only keeping, instead of that story with its final knowledge, the images and ideas that first emerged for me when I began writing, that continue to burn and blaze and show, that I can't let go. For it is the beginning to which, always, I want to return—to live inside and stay. In the account of a man who, when he stepped in the door, seemed to touch the ceiling, he was so tall. His voice yelling out to his family that he was back and them all then come gathering in. A man who, as far as his family were concerned, was connected to all others, to the world, to the country he was born to, and its animals and its ways. Who knew its hidden places and gullies, could go there to them and come home again. That story, of the man I wanted to be one day when I grew up, and who I longed for, and whose sons, to my great blessing, did count me for a time among their number. That man. Him. Gone out as not belonging maybe, and part of no system or plan—but coming back anyhow, returned from the past and the dark and the violence. Unarmed and unscathed. Royal.

'It is lonely being a young man sent abroad to fight,' she said.

My sister called to tell me about a dream she'd had. 'I have to give you all the details while they're still fresh in my mind,' she said. Sophie is like that. Everything that happens must be followed by a conversation—it's always event plus discussion, event plus discussion—even if the 'everything' is just some rag bag of images hauled up from her unconscious and set before her while she is asleep. 'It was about animals,' she said, 'the dream, and it took place in a stable—but not a stable, actually,' she corrected herself, 'the building the animals were sheltered in was really the ruins of a once grand house.'

'That's pretty detailed,' I said. 'The part about the house ...'

'Yes. And it was beautiful, Mary. Queen Anne, I think, or something like that but it had fallen into disrepair and now it was full of cows and sheep and some kind of long-legged llama, though a llama with the stubborn snout of a pig.'

'Another detail,' I said, 'of your dream.'

'Exactly. And there were animals with beaks—or bills, rather, as though they were geese, but they were nothing like geese because they were tall. Like an extinct New Zealand moa, that tall and flightless bird, but with wool, not feathers. Do you see what I'm getting at, Mary? The dream was strange.'

'Strange,' I said. 'I'll say. What had you been thinking, during the day, I mean, before you went to sleep? Had you had a strange encounter? Met someone? Had you eaten something funny?'

'Funny?' said Sophie. 'No, no,' she said. *No, no* … in that cross, impatient way she has, that doesn't mean she's cross, only that she wants to get on with things and can't bear any diversions. 'No, no. It was just a dream full of animals, that's all. It hadn't come *from* anywhere, it was an imaginary figment … about domestic animals, herds or flocks or whatever, crowding this stable, I mean, the place was dense with livestock, *dense,* Mary. Yet I walked right through them.'

'Is it something to do with Christmas?' I said, though Christmas was a while off. 'Stable, animals …'

'I simply walked through them,' my sister said, as though she hadn't heard me. 'I walked into the centre of this herd of animals, into the middle of the group. I went right in and then …'

'Then?'

'Well, I turned around and came out,' she said. 'There was a dear little calf who was eating some kind of gruel from a pink bowl and it gave me a wild-eyed and frightened look as I walked past, but of course I wasn't going to hurt it.'

'Goodness,' I said. 'What does it all mean, I wonder?'

'Who knows,' Sophie said. 'Only I wanted to tell you because it was so interesting, so visual. Like one of your stories, Mary. At first the animals seemed scary, one of the llama creatures with the pig's nose tried to butt me, but I just kept moving carefully through them all. I'd been intimidated, of course, so many of them, you know, in such a tightly packed crowd—'

'Crowd?' I said. 'That's a strange way to describe—'

'Oh well, flock then. Herd. What I said before … Whatever. Don't be such a damn *writer,* Mary. Why must it be always "words, words" with you? Getting everything down in just the right, the exact, kind of way ...' I laughed then. My sister often makes me laugh. Her somehow brutal take on life. Her impatience with 'Art'. She's a dentist, an orthodontist actually, and the idea that someone might write stories, that one might do this for a living, is as ridiculous to her as the idea of looking inside people's mouths all day is ridiculous to me. Sure, my sister is a total success at what she does—she has her own practice; that's her name on a brass plate on the door and I'm always hitting her up for loans and she always seems to have money to spare—but I have to say, apart from the massive income generated by people's crooked and overcrowded teeth, I can't understand for a minute how she is able to do what she does, and, for her part, she can't begin to get her head around why I would do nothing but sit in front of a laptop all day writing articles and advertisements and the occasional short story for magazines that generally don't want to publish them. Still, there's something about us both that makes people think we're kind of similar. Her dream, my words. It's all there in that phrase 'event plus discussion', I suppose.

We talked a bit more. It was our mother's birthday and we were planning to take her on a trip to Rome—and Sophie also told me about her new boyfriend who she'd decided she was going to break up with because there 'wasn't much to him', as she put it. And then she'd asked about my husband and me and the boys and I said we were all fine.

'Bye, then. Give Robert my love,' she said.

'I will,' I replied. 'And talk to Mum again, will you? About that hotel? I think the bells will drive her crazy even though she does want to be that close to St Peter's. They'll start ringing them really early in the morning and I don't think she's factored that in. Also the processions. Catholics are mad for that sort of thing.'

'I'll talk to her,' Sophie promised. 'And you think about my dream, will you?' she finished by saying. 'There's something going on there and I'd like to get to the bottom of it. I've never given any kind of animal a moment's thought before, as you know.'

'Fine,' I said, and then we hung up and I went off to the kitchen to tidy up after the rampage that is Hamish and Davey going off to school, but all the while, it's true, I was thinking about my sister's dream, that stable—sorry, 'house'—the herd of animals and so on—and sure enough, I couldn't help it, I started thinking, too, about a story that might come from all that ...

A few weeks earlier, my dear friend Alison, who I hadn't heard from in ages had come around to the house in a kind of panic. 'The people next door have a cat and they're not taking care of it and they've abandoned it is what I think,' she'd said—all in a breathless rush because her car was double-parked right outside and she'd wanted me to get straight into it and drive back with her to our old neighbourhood so that we could confront the situation that very morning. 'It's not even a cat they're mistreating, Mary,' she said. 'It's a kitten, a tiny, tiny kitten. They leave it on its own in the flat all day. When I'm up on the roof terrace I can hear it, through a window which they keep open. It's in there, crying and crying. Then I woke up this morning and it was the first thing I could hear, this desperate little sound, like—' she composed her face and closed her eyes. 'Mi-aow,' she said, drawing out the vowels so that she sounded like a sad and desperate little kitten herself. 'Mi-aaa-ow!' she cried again, piteously. 'We have to do something, Mary. Come over to the flat with me now.'

Alison is someone I have known for a long time. The flat to which she was referring was my old flat, the flat I'd bought in another life it may as well have been, before I'd met Robert and had the boys—when Alison and I used to be neighbours. We used to see each other most days back then, discuss various ideas for the future, plan a range of different projects and events. The day I'd moved in I'd gone up onto the roof terrace—which was the reason I'd decided to buy the flat in the first place—to look at the view and Alison had been up there on her terrace, right next door, watering the plants.

'Oh, hello,' she said.

Some friendships start that way: Oh, hello. Well, hello, back. And off you go as though someone has fired a gun. So it was with us: Two roof terraces, two flats … We were like kids with jam. All we had to do to see each other was go upstairs and call over the wall. 'Do you want to come next door?' 'Yeah!' 'Shall we have a party?' 'Why not!' Just thinking about that chapter of my life makes me see how it could be another whole story in itself—a book of stories, or a TV series, even: *Alison and Mary on the Roof with Friends. What Alison and Mary Did Next* etc, etc. The whole set-up was made for fiction.

This story, though, the one I'm writing down now, has me standing there at my front door with Alison's car double-parked outside the gate and Alison's voice high and strained with worry because of a kitten she has heard though never seen—still she knows it's 'tiny' and it's been 'abandoned' and it's 'crying and crying' … And oh yes, I get it. I totally get it. One of the first things Alison and I talked about when we met that day on the roof was how we loved pets—cats in particular—and how she'd had an extremely affection- ate old tom cat called Walter who had died five years ago but she still missed him.

'Listen,' I said to her in the car as we were driving over there, to my old flat, so that we could figure things out. 'How do you know they're neglecting the kitten, really? There could be someone in the flat all day, playing with it, feeding it, and the kitten just likes to mew. Some cats are like that. They like to make a sound. Siamese cats, for example. And Charlie, you know, she gives me little miaows all day, in greeting, when I'm working and she jumps on the desk—'

'This is nothing like Charlie,' Alison said with great certainty, her eyes fixed on the road ahead while rummaging on the dashboard for cigarettes and driving very fast. She could speak with that kind of authority about my cat because Charlie was given to me by Alison years ago as a birthday present, a black and confident little rescue kitten from the local PetsWatch with whom Alison is in constant contact. She'd found out from the manager there that a ten-week-old kitten was about to be put down because of an asthma condition—and we had a garden, I was home all day, the boys were gentle with animals … It wasn't even that close to my birthday, actually, but things were sliding with my writing and I was having trouble getting back into it once the boys had started school and Alison knew all along that Charlie would help. She's a lucky black cat in every way; even that asthma condition that so threatened her life disappeared within days of her moving in.

'Nothing like,' Alison repeated emphatically now. 'This young cat is MISERABLE, Mary. The people next door are NEVER in. In fact, sometimes they are not in for days and days at a time. I know that because I've been watching the flat. I see people leave …' She paused, as though for effect, but in fact she was inhaling and exhaling cigarette smoke. 'And I DON'T see them return.'

I knew, of course I did—and I didn't need any of her talking in capital letters to tell me—by the smoking, the smoking in the car and the smoking while driving, that this was a pretty serious situation. Alison only ever smoked if she was very worried about something or extremely excited. Now she drew heavily on her cigarette, held her breath dramatically, and, after a beat, exhaled again, all the while driving in her expert way. 'I am talking DAYS at a time …' she said, flicking the ash out the open window and not taking her eyes from the road. 'DAYS, Mary.'

By now we were just about back in the old neighbourhood. We're not that far apart, Alison and I, but because we are no longer exactly next door to each other, we feel the difference. Still, it had taken only five minutes or so to cross the space between where I live now and where I lived then, and the time had passed without us coming to any sort of conclusion.

'Maybe they have someone come in?' I said. 'To feed the kitten? A person who you don't see arriving ...?'

'I hardly think so,' Alison flicked her cigarette out the window and pulled into a parking space right outside her building. 'No. Your tenants have simply left an animal on its own, to fend for itself. It's thoughtless and wicked and that's why you and I are here now. We're going to go in there and confront them. It's your flat, after all, Mary. You have the right to be authorial in this situation.'

Authorial, eh? I thought. Well that's an interesting word. Writer. Author. Event. Discussion ... etc, etc ... Though all I said was, 'Yes, but—'

'Come on,' Alison said, commanding me. There were two spots of high colour on her delicate cheekbones. 'It's not negotiable, this situation. I know you feel about this the way I do.' She was right, of course. The minute Alison had told me about the kitten I'd felt sick. Who could do that sort of thing? Be careless? Cruel, even? And it was true, too, as Alison had said: It was my flat. After getting married, Sophie and Robert and my mother had told me not to sell and to hold onto the place as an investment, sort of. It was the practical thing to do. I'd managed to buy at a time when property prices weren't so crazy in London and I'd thought I was going to have a successful career in advertising so I could afford the down payment and monthly mortgage costs. Then, by the time I'd left the agency,

I'd met Robert and published a little collection of short stories and life seemed to have changed. Robert and I decided to get married; I started writing articles and advertorials as my day job; we moved to somewhere with a garden. 'But you shouldn't sell that flat,' everyone had said, Alison included, because she had Sophie on the phone to her all the time telling her how much sense it made for me to keep it. During that entire period Sophie had been in training, first as a dentist, then orthodontist, and was getting herself set up in her own practice. Already it was clear she was going to have a very successful career and would manage the practical side of her life with a great deal of foresight and efficiency. My not selling the flat, I know, is the only thing I've done of which Sophie thoroughly approves. She loves the flat herself, and she and Alison adore each other.

'Let's go in there now,' Alison said. 'It will be necessary to use your keys.'

There comes a time in all short stories when the register of the narrative shifts: a character is introduced who changes things, or the mood alters, the tone, the story has a different feel. Up until now, everything had been quite straightforward—the conversations, the explanations—but at this moment, the paragraph above sitting out there on its own like that ... I suppose you could say this was the moment in this story when I realised things were coming together in a way that a reader might find quite alarming. Because the idea of me using my keys, getting them out and exercising—what?—my landlord's rights? My—as Alison had put it—authorial rights? Well, it changed things, that's for sure. Things now coming together with a view to—what? Breaking and entering? Trespassing? Alison and I wilfully letting ourselves into a property that was legally tenanted and behaving as though it was our own? Walking into someone else's

home with no consideration of their own position of legal entitle-
ment, but thinking only of cat rescue, animal rights? Yes. Breaking
and entering. That was what Alison was proposing, alright. Though
we had keys, my set of keys, still: We would be involved, completely,
in what could only be described as a criminal act.

'I can't use my key,' I said. 'The Harrisons are tenants. They live
there. They've been there for years. I can't just let myself in.'

'Knock on the door then.'

'Well ...'

'Knock on the door first. For goodness' sake, Mary!'

By now we were at the front door of my flat and Alison's voice
was high and wild. 'For goodness' sake!' she said again. 'It's a tiny
kitten! All rules are off!'

'Well ...' I was sounding uncertain when really I wasn't uncertain
at all. There was no way I'd been talked into this. I knew exactly what
Alison meant and I was in full agreement. I knocked three times.
'It's a desperate situation,' I said. Then I put the key in the lock and
turned it, opened the door. Alison and I stepped inside.

So 'Broke'. So 'Entered'. In fact those exact words had come up in
an article I'd been writing earlier that week. It was a piece about cars
for weddings, for a certain kind of newspaper that ran pages on that
sort of thing, at certain times of the year, more of an advert, really,
for car hire companies that had already paid the paper a substantial
fee for the opportunity to be featured in a quite glamorous page that
would look like an editorial. I'd created an exciting angle that gave
the wedding transport theme a lift by describing it as something racy,
as though weddings were a kind of illicit or even illegal activity that
might require a getaway car. I'd created subheads along the lines of
'Hit and Run' and 'Leaving the Scene of the Crime', and I'd written
a sentence that ran something like—'Now you've gone for broke and

entered the wild world of matrimony, fixed those vows in ink and headed back up the aisle, you're gonna need the kind of car that can get you out of that place quick, baby. Rushdons of Harpenden have a damn fine Ferrari in traffic-stopping scarlet that you can really break bad in …' etc, etc. It was all very *Tatler*—a magazine I'd worked at before going in for advertising that had trained me in a certain kind of writing style that I could pull out whenever I needed to—a sort of fizzy, fast sentence that went down well across most of the broadsheets for any style piece that they might want to run. So 'broke' and 'entered' … Yes. These were, that week, particularly familiar words to me.

Alison and I went into the narrow hall, and straight away, there it was, we heard it, a forsaken little miaow. 'See?' said Alison, and again she was right. For that sound wasn't anything like the miaow from Charlie when I'd picked her up in my arms that morning, as I picked her up every morning after the boys had left for school, just to hold her for a moment, look into her clever little black face, and say hello. Charlie's miaow was like a one-stop open-your-mouth-wide-and-show-me-all-your-teeth kind of miaow, perfunctory and polite all at once—which is what it was. Miaow: Hello to you as well. Now put me down. This other sort of miaow, that I was hearing was pitiful and insistent and thin, a needy, mournful sound repeating over and over: Miaow. Miaow. Miaow. The sound of a young animal in trouble.

'See?' Alison said again. 'Aren't you glad we've come?'

I was. In fact, I was more than glad, I was shockingly relieved. Quite apart from my immediate concern about the kitten's welfare, I'd seen straight away that there was something very, very wrong here, in my flat. As we walked up the stairs what I can only describe as material detritus was piled thick and high around us, boxes, clothes, bags of paper rubbish, books and magazines, shoes and boots strewn everywhere. There was electrical equipment, televisions and stereos.

There were packages of unopened clothes, T-shirts and jerseys and trousers, still in the cellophane wrappers in which they'd been delivered or else half unwrapped and left strewn among cardboard packaging. Thank goodness I'd listened to my dear friend and come here with her. This flat wasn't like my flat at all, the flat I'd rented years ago to the responsible and orderly Harrisons. It was like the repository of some second-hand shop or warehouse or storage unit with everything just dumped any old how; stuff piled all the way up the stairs, and, as we got to it, in the kitchen and in the living room as well, and more so. There, I could see boxes stacked up against the walls, against the windows, like a barricade, like a defence, with more plastic crates sitting on top of one another, big boxes, little boxes, some open, with more brand new electrical items inside—toasters and CD players and radios—and others with books and gardening implements, some of the boxes closed fast, and unopened even, others split wide and full of what looked like breakables, all wrapped in crumpled newspaper as though someone were trying to pack up and leave. There was barely a foot of space on the floor on which to stand—and all the time, as I was seeing all of this ... chaos ... there was the sad insistent mewing of a kitten in distress, coming from ... where? From upstairs or inside or under one of the boxes? From behind one of the piles of books or shoes? Who could tell? My stomach lurched. This was no kind of place to leave a pet. This was no kind of place for anyone.

On top of all this, I was having another kind of strange, lurching feeling that came from being back in the flat after so much time away. It had been many years, many, many years since I'd packed away my things and had gone to live with Robert and then married him. Since then, I'd had a lettings company managing the property for me and they took care of every single aspect of running the place. They had introduced the tenants to the property, organised their move in, and for years at a time I would hear nothing at all. Occasionally, the agency told me, they were replacing this, or the Harrisons had asked for that, and all I had to do was say, 'Yes, that seems fine,' and the rental went straight into my account every month after they'd deducted their fee. All those years had passed, and I'd been away, not thinking much about this flat, living my life with my husband and my two boys, yet now here I was, back inside the rooms of what had once been my home. My first-time buy—as the estate agents used to call all the flats like mine back then—one of those endless conversions that run the length and breadth of London, making of an Edwardian or Victorian two-storey terrace house a set of two or three flats, of the grand stucco-fronted villas and mansions even more. All those flats, those homes. And all of them pretty much the same when you got into them, and most of them quite a lot like mine, probably, with nice rooms and big windows—only my first-time buy had that roof terrace. And the roof terrace had changed everything. That 'Oh, hello' of Alison's, remember? The first day I moved in? And my 'hello' back. Miaow. Miaow. As neat as my own little black cat's greeting in the morning.

Only look at it now. The flat was barely recognisable as a place where I had once lived. That sense of stuff everywhere, the amount of that stuff … it meant something sad and awful and desperate, something lingering and out of control was being enacted within those once-lovely rooms. Something was very, very wrong. Alison and I stood side by side, not speaking even. We couldn't speak. And all the time there was the pitiful crying, the mewing, of a young cat inside something, or under something, caught in something? We went through the kitchen and sitting room calling and looking, though we could barely get into these rooms for boxes and boots, army boots, I could see maybe ten pairs of them in the sitting room and all brand new. What was going on here? I felt sick. In the sitting room, by one of the long windows, was a StairMaster—a StairMaster for goodness' sake, and next to it a rowing machine … Alison and I couldn't really get into that room at all, into that once pretty little sitting room. It looked like no kind of room I'd ever been in before in my life, no kind of room anyone could live in. It looked like a wreck of a room, an abandoned blown-up place, a disaster zone. For a few moments, standing there on the landing I was so stunned by all that I'd seen that I couldn't move, couldn't think what I was there for, even. Then I heard that little squeaky miaow again and Alison gripped my forearm and there in front of us, sitting on a box, was a very young cat. She looked up at us and opened her mouth as though she was going to let out a loud extended yowl but instead gave just a little squeak. 'Well, hello,' Alison said. Her voice was very low and calm and soothing. 'Just look at you' she said, and the kitten closed her eyes and opened them again, quite slowly. 'Just look at you,' Alison said to her again. 'Aren't you pretty?'

The kitten can't have been more than four months old. She was pale ginger and black with a white bib, a dainty little tortoiseshell with four long white socks and a black patch over one eye and a ginger nose that gave her a jaunty and clever appearance. She regarded Alison and then me for a moment, that 'Oh, hello' had interested her, then turned, bounced up onto another box and in a blink, she was gone, hidden—underneath the same box or tucked in between the fixings of one of the machines behind it—a liquidiser or a juicer or Magimix. We heard a squeak from somewhere there in the darkness created by that piled-together stuff, then another long pitiful miaow that made me cry out, 'No! No! No!' and a voice came down from upstairs:

'Who's there?'

Alison and I looked at each other.

We'd forgotten all about the tenants. Since I'd knocked on the door, turned the key and gone inside I hadn't given another thought to 'Breaking and Entering'. I'd forgotten all about being the landlord, who should have phoned first, via the lettings company, to arrange for an appointment to meet; I'd forgotten all about the rules for that sort of thing. And now, here we were: two people, illegal. One of them the proprietor, who should have more of a feeling of propriety about breaking and entering than anyone. One, a person who lived right next door to the house being broken into and entered, and who would from then on be known forever, by the victims of the crime, no longer as a neighbour but as a criminally oriented person who could not be trusted.

'You WHAT?' Robert would say. 'You just let yourself in without knocking?'

'I did knock.'

'And walked right in? It's not your flat, Mary! You don't live there! You rent it out! To your tenants, good tenants, who've been there for years. You broke into their home, you and Alison, and all because of some notion about a cat. Your behaviour was frankly illegal.' By now he was repeating himself—that phrase: 'Frankly illegal' … It would come up in our many discussions about the situation, over and over again. Robert shook his head. 'You two,' he said.

This conversation, me telling Robert what had happened, describing the many details of the incident in full, would take place days later when the whole issue of the kitten had been resolved and her story could be spoken of freely and without fear of consequence.

'It was a rescue mission, remember,' Alison said to Robert then. And she tweaked his nose. 'You silly,' she said. 'You would have done the same …'

'I certainly would not have,' Robert said, but he was smiling. He and I were both over at Alison's for drinks and she'd made margaritas. She and Robert were both smoking away like it was the eighties, with an air of great recklessness—he, because he'd given up, she, because she was excited, very, having achieved such a satisfactory outcome, a most happy and successful ending, to the story of a little neglected cat for whom, quite easily, things may not have turned out so well.

'You would have done the same,' Alison said again, taking a slug from her margarita and a great big puff from her Marlboro Light.

'The kitten is adorable and needed a new home. That,' she said, 'was clear.'

'And that,' I chimed in, 'is what has happened. She now has a new home. A loving lovely home. All's well that ends well. Although ...' I looked at Alison. 'Well, not quite ...'

'Not quite,' she agreed, suddenly sober. 'Not quite at all ...'

Because nothing is quite as simple as an ending, is it? Not quite as straightforward as 'event plus discussion, event plus discussion', not quite as clear-cut as that—even though people like my sister are keen on such ideas, that everything can be figured out. So it was that when that voice had come down to us from upstairs, the 'Who's there?' Alison and I hadn't been expecting, well, things took a turn then, over the next few minutes and days that followed, took a very different turn, really, events casting a different light on the particular story we'd been involved in so far that changed it—another of those moments I wrote about before when 'the register of the narrative shifts.'

'You're just a kitten yourself,' Alison would say to him when some weeks had passed, and she had got to know him better, the young man who came down the stairs that day when he heard the voices of two strangers in his home. 'You need someone to look after you,' Alison would say.

For he was no more than a boy, the young man who had been living in my old flat, who had been there for just under a year, he said, first as a guest of the Harrisons, and then, when they'd moved away for a period, as a tenant of theirs, living alone pretty much all of the time in preparation for going overseas, to Iraq, though why there, I have no idea, when I thought that war was supposed to be over and all the soldiers had come home. He had been in the flat on his own for all that time and month by month had been gathering around him the things that he thought he would need. Buying things. Collecting things. Accumulating, stockpiling. And yes, Alison had been right, he'd been out of the flat for long stretches, going on military exercises with his unit, going out in the country to barracks somewhere so he could learn to pick up a rifle and a pack and go back into Iraq for some kind of 'activity', the newspapers were describing it as, 'a period of training and preparation', they said. The Harrisons hadn't been there for more than ten months, it turned out. They were away in Brussels for work, and so in that time the stuff in the flat that we'd seen that day, so much of it army stuff—the boxes of boots, uniform supplies and kit and other stuff that he thought he might need—had proliferated, accumulated. All those things that he'd been buying and collecting, ordering online every day, stuff, more stuff … it had built up around him, all around him … and here he was, and here was all this stuff—and he was about to leave. The sublet from the Harrisons was only good for the year they were in Brussels, his stay was only ever going to be temporary, he said. Because he was in the army and due for deployment, any day now, he'd be sent off.

'Don't worry,' he'd said. 'The Harrisons are still officially your tenants, they're coming back … Don't worry about that—'

By then he was down the stairs, and we'd all introduced ourselves and taken seats on various boxes. The kitten had come out from where she'd been hiding and was sitting in his lap, purring.

'It's not the tenancy I'm thinking about right now,' I said. 'All that's fine, the flat ... No. What I'm worried about ...' My voice trailed off, it was an awkward situation. I didn't have a right to be there, let alone make personal remarks about the circumstances I'd uncovered on my visit, and the kitten, it has to be said, seemed very happy sitting on his knee. It was hardly my role to intervene. But Alison simply asked him, in a forthright way, 'Who is going to look after your kitten if you're going away?'

The young man, the boy—he was only a boy— gave me a look. I thought for a minute he was going to cry. His name was Anthony, his mother had named him Anthony after a saint, as I now know from my mother, when I was describing the whole situation to her, because she's so familiar with that sort of thing, saints and churches and the Catholic faith and so on, there was that trip to Rome being planned, remember?

'Can I say here that not for one moment did that young man make me feel like a criminal,' I said to Robert, when Alison and I were explaining everything to him over cocktails. For not for one moment after we'd broken into his home and behaved 'frankly illegally', as Robert had described it, after Anthony had called down the stairs, 'Who's there?' and I'd replied, trying to make the situation seem quite usual and ordinary, by calling back up the stairs, 'Don't worry, it's just me. The landlady.' 'Not for one moment did he make Alison and me feel awkward about our situation,' I said.

'He welcomed us being there,' Alison said. 'It was a relief, you see. That he had people to talk to, that we'd come in and now he had people helping him decide what he was going to do. Up until then he'd been confused. All those things he'd collected, sitting there, pressing in around him ...'

131

And to this extent, writing this down as some kind of a story, I think of my sister Sophie's dream … Those animals packed in tightly, as she dreamed them, penned in at the forecourt of some grand house or whatever, her feelings in the dream, of both fear and of fearlessness, being enclosed herself with strange creatures and then going in to be among them … So my old flat with stuff everywhere, so tightly packed in that I could barely get to the sink in the kitchen for water, after I'd said to Anthony, 'Where is your kitten's water bowl and I can fill it?' and, more firmly, 'Where is her food?' For here was a situation not unlike a dream, maybe: Fear and fearlessness set among confusion; a kitten in the arms of a lonely boy who, in a few days, was due to be shipped abroad to one of these wars of ours that never seem to be over. 'A period of training and preparation'—what does that even mean? When you think of it, the whole thing is like some kind of strange unbelievable story that takes place at night …

'My mother has been coming in to feed her while I've been away,' Anthony said to us. 'And sometimes a friend of my mother's …'

'But when you're gone?' Alison pressed him.

'I don't know,' he admitted. He looked down at the kitten's face and tickled her between her ears.

'You will have to let us help you,' I said, gently then.

'Will you?' Anthony turned to Alison. 'Can you?'

Alison nodded, mouthed the word Yes, in a calming, soothing way. Yes. Yes. Yes.

'And that "yes" was the beginning of a process that lasted for several days,' I said to Robert, putting the whole thing together in sequence for him, that night at Alison's, when we had the margaritas. I told him all about the various conversations and deliberations, first between Alison and everyone at PetsWatch. 'They were brilliant, of course, and had loads of advice,' said Alison. 'They told me we'd done absolutely, absolutely the right thing.' Then between Alison and Anthony, obviously, figuring out exactly what they'd do. 'I had to take it very slowly,' Alison said, 'because she was his kitten, naturally, and he loved her.' And then, yes, there were the conversations between Alison and me. Long and detailed discussions that ended, as I explained to Robert, with Alison announcing to me, 'Hurrah! Success! We have Happy Ever After!'—when Anthony had left for Iraq and 'Squeaky' now renamed 'Dot' was gifted by Alison to my sister Sophie, who said that though she thought she never liked cats, had never wanted one, she could now see that she did, from the moment Alison gathered up the little tortoiseshell and placed her in my sister's arms, and my sister looked down at the kitten and then up at Alison and smiled.

'Remember, he was only lonely,' Alison reminded me when we were talking about everything again, as a kind of coda, and I was telling her that I was thinking about writing a short story all about what had happened, about Anthony and the flat and even the dream. 'I've told him about Sophie, of course,' Alison said. 'I text him, and he texts back. And I've been sending him lots of pictures by phone to Baghdad'—and she described them: Dot sleeping in Sophie's garden. Dot chasing her tail, chasing a butterfly, drinking milk from a dish … 'Doing things cats should do,' Alison had said to Robert, as she poured him another margarita, taking a drag from her cigarette. 'Not being alone in a flat all day. The pictures comfort Anthony, I think,' she said.

Which is about where I get to by the end of all this: her saying that to Robert, and saying then, just as she was topping up his glass, that line that I have used for the title of this story. That, to her mind, that's what the whole thing had been about—the buying of everything, the getting in of all the stuff, the piles of boxes and the mail order and keeping it all close …

'He loved that kitten,' Alison said. 'He was lonely and the kitten helped him. Of course he didn't want to think about the day he was going to have to leave her. To leave. So he didn't think about it.'

'But that's where we came in,' I said.

'That's where we came in,' Alison answered.

And Sophie, when I called her today and read her this whole story out loud, agreed. 'I can see, weirdly, why you started everything with my dream as well,' she said. 'Of course he needed to gather those things around him and couldn't let any of it go. And of course, too, you both needed to go in there and sort it out. She's right, Alison is right. It is lonely being a young man sent abroad to fight,' she said.

The Round Pool

He had gone back to the place where he used to fish but it had all changed there. As though, overnight, someone had come in and put up notices on fencelines and gates, had posted signs—'No Unauthorised Vehicles'—'No Right of Way'—'Private Road'—that was how it had seemed. As though it had happened that quickly, when of course who knew how long the notices had been up, and the fences. It had been years since he'd been back to the estate and the river, and it would have been occurring slowly, no doubt, all this. The owners could have done anything to the place in the time since the lodge had been left closed up and with no keeper since Johnny had left. No. Not since then. And that had been long enough ago.

And where had they ended up, anyhow, Johnny and Sarah? And why hadn't he kept in touch with them, that he might have known? He'd thought about that, sure enough, while he'd been driving up that morning, coming in off the back road, had wondered then about the keeper and his wife and about the care they had taken looking after things here, the land and water, and why hadn't he bothered to find out where they'd gone? But there was a lot you'd think he might have done that he hadn't. And as he'd come in along the old way, over the first hill, and the second, all that had been in his mind, his carelessness. Cresting the second hill and with the flatlands laid out ahead of him, pale green and grey and marked all over with thin lochs and burns and rivers … Thinking about the way he'd learned not to bother about anyone, to ask after them, or think about them; the kind of man he'd become. That had been in his mind, sure enough—yet it had only been later, when he'd seen the first sign, that the boy in him had risen up and he'd felt wretched then, at the sight of it. For he had known himself at that moment to be the boy again, not the man, and he'd had to stop the car.

There had been no signs in the past, no gates. There'd been no fences, even, when some might have said you could have done with a fence, maybe, to give indication of how you were moving across that great expanse of land. A fence might have articulated the shape of the place, distances, when there'd been only ever the river running along to the left as you were coming in to give a sense of direction. There'd always been the lovely turn and different colours of the river. The parts where it was deep or still or broken into falls and then dropping down, these had been printed onto him, and the parts where it widened out again with little beaches carved out at the edges, and the wild thyme that used to grow up against the water there, and the heather and the sound of bees in high summer. So, really … he'd had no need of a fence. He had always known where he was here. And being back again, as he'd decided to come back and have a look at the place after the years away, to be near the water, that he might hear the sound of it running over the rocks, stilling, then taking up again … How all this had come in upon him when he'd stopped for a while after opening that first gate and had stood and listened. Thinking then about how he had always been able to rely on the river to give indication, so you might know how much further it would be to the Long Pool, say, or the Rock, to the Elbow or the Dark Water or the Round … All the lovely places where you might have found a fish waiting for you. A beautiful salmon. Then he'd driven on.

Gate or no gate, sign or no sign, it had been good to be back. To be driving down through the estate and remembering the water, to be near it and to be thinking about fishing again, and about the clean black colour of the river with its peaty gold in the shallows but rich and dark where it was deep, it had been reassuring, yes, it had. As though an easing, somehow, of all that had gone on in the time he'd been away, to be thinking instead only about where he might have had a try with his rod, the fly he might have used in weather that was grey but bright. For there had been also, when he'd arrived at that first gate, sign of recent rain. It had been warm and with a steady breeze, but rain had fallen in the night before, or early that morning and so the right weather exactly for fishing the river. 'Like this, Robbie, remember?' As he'd always been told. That there'd be one particular fly good for this sort of day, or 'No, try this,' on another. To think in that way about temperature, the speed of the water … Of course he'd remembered. He'd got out of the car at a second gate and had scanned the sky again for weather. Now, he'd thought, it would be fine.

The first gate hadn't been closed, despite the awful sign. 'No Vehicles Beyond This Point' had been printed in red letters on a white board and attached to a post, but the gate itself had been pulled back enough that he'd been able to drive through quite easily. This second one, though, he'd had to undo. There'd been a bit of a fuss with it, two bolts, but he'd managed to pull the thing open and fix it back again after him, and though he'd felt the wrench of having to do that, open and close a gate attached to a fenceline that had never been there before, he'd decided by then he wouldn't let himself mind about it. He'd become that boy again, you see? Thinking about the day. Thinking about the beautiful fish. About the salmon lying there somewhere in a still pool, just resting, as though waiting for him. So he had driven on down the hill and onto the lovely flat where the river had always opened up so nicely and had even seemed to hear it speaking to itself as he had always thought when he was a boy that the river might do, in a language of its own: *Here's everything you need* ... As though it was a companion, was how it had always felt, running alongside him, the murmuring sound of it reassuring him and making him feel confident and strong ... And it had been true, hadn't it? That nothing else had seemed to matter to him then?

Is why he had been able to keep driving that day on a road much smoothed out and tarred over in a way it had never been in the past, with none of the rough gravel and potholes that had always been there, and yet he hadn't even seemed to notice it. After he'd opened the second gate he'd simply passed right through and driven on, and with the windows down to smell the sweet air of the place only to remember by then, yes, all the times of being here as a boy with his father, and as a young man. All those years. All that time. And, *Everything* ... Yes. And so thinking again, what had happened to him? That he had allowed it? To let this go? Why would the boy in him not have stopped him from turning away? For by then all that had been in his mind had been memories of the place, and the fullness of the hours, the days. Only remembering everything that he'd had, his father bringing him here when he was young and growing up and how he'd had to learn about it, this part of the country, and the right ways of going about things, the right way to behave. And of course his father had been getting older with each year, all the time getting older, but still the two of them had been able to fish together, moving along the different parts of the river with every inch of it so known to them and held so carefully in their minds that later, after his father's death, he'd wanted to come with friends here, to show them how it was, the lovely water and its land, though they hadn't liked it and they hadn't come back. And he had come with his wife and children but they'd not liked it either. It had been too far away for them, is what they'd all said, the friends, the wife, and for those reasons, and more, he'd not come back here himself—and again, why? He might have asked himself that question many years ago, but he had not. In the way he'd never wanted to ask himself questions about who he was or what his life had been like, or think too hard altogether about what he had done and not done or what he could have done, perhaps, to change things for himself. So that when he had finally returned, as though he might have picked up where he'd left off, it was no wonder that he had been alone.

'Where have you brought me?' Margaret had said that to him when he'd first introduced her to the way of things here, when they were newly married and his father had still been alive, and all the old fishing party together. She'd turned to him, at the door of the lodge, before they'd gone in. 'My God,' she'd said, and he'd always remembered the sound of her voice at that moment, a tone in it he'd not heard before. He'd wanted to run from her then. And the way she'd said, too, 'Never, ever am I coming here again,' later, when he'd tried again with her, to bring her when the children had been little and they might have liked it here, mightn't they? He'd thought so. 'But they don't like it,' Margaret had said, when they'd come back, three or four years later, after that other time. 'This is no place for a child.'

No place indeed. He had found himself laughing, there in the car on his own, with the river over to the left of him where he couldn't see it but still he'd felt it beside him. He'd only laughed out loud, on his own like an idiot, remembering her saying that to him. Now that he was back here again and knowing how lovely it was, feeling it working upon him, the fineness of the hills and the moor and the clear air … No wonder it had only made him want to laugh. At her, her stupidity. Because who had she been? That she'd thought there was nothing to this country, nothing in it, only emptiness. And he'd laughed at himself too, for that matter. Because who had he been? To be so in awe of her? Married to her, even? Had children with her who he never saw? He'd thought about that, too, in the car that day—because what had he thought he'd been doing? Thinking he would have had that kind of life? It had been long enough ago, he'd thought, but yes, for sure, his wife's foolishness could only ever have been his own. And it didn't matter now anyhow. The way she'd been, the way he'd been with her and with the children. And it didn't matter either that in all the time since he'd been alone. The important thing, he'd told himself, coming along the flat where the river would be wide, was that he himself had been able to return, had recovered the desire to be here. That he'd believed, yes he really had, that just by being here again he might be restored.

And it had been so very beautiful, that afternoon. The air grey and warm, and a strong sun would come through in time—is what he'd thought as well—that it would be a fine, fine evening later, oh yes. He'd gone through that in his mind also, remembering evenings in the past, and them all sitting out at the front of the lodge with a drink and the sun on their faces; the way he would come in on them, so happy gathered there together, talking about the day and the fish they'd seen and caught or not caught … And he had imagined, even as he'd had to stop at a third gate and it had been locked, how the evening ahead for him would have still been a good one, and fine in the way the evenings had always been fine in the old days, and endless, somehow. Is how it had always felt. As a boy, and as a young man. That he wouldn't need to worry about anything or have to learn what it was to be someone who would be disappointed in himself and alone. That the evening instead would be there for him when the day was over. And that it would be endless and fine.

The third gate had been truly barred against him, though. This time it was a gate that had been properly locked, not just closed and looking as though it was padlocked but with two sliding bolts and padlocks and another chain that also locked, and another of the big metal signs. He'd had to leave the car there. It had taken a minute or two for him to realise it. That he couldn't drive any further and would need to turn off the road and onto the edge of the moor and just leave the car. But then, as easily, he had done that, left it, and had started the long walk to where the Round Pool would be waiting for him. Because even then, with that gate and the sign 'Authorised Access Only', he hadn't been deterred, had he? Though he might have been? For look all around him. The grey green land of the place with its loveliness and distant hills as though he could touch them, the sunlight, a warm steady breeze and the river down to the left of the track as he knew it would be. It had turned into a glorious, glorious day.

And of course by then all that had been on his mind was how he might have had a line out over a bit of river, to get up to the Round and see for himself how things might be there now, still set on getting there, you see. Still believing. And so not minding the long walk to the pool for he'd been looking forward to this moment for … what? Weeks? Months? Longer, even—so why, he'd thought, should he be deterred? There'd been no one around to tell him otherwise. No one to have been involved in running the estate altogether, as far as he'd been able to see. He'd called the office number earlier in the morning and there'd been no answer, and no one in down at the village either, at the building there that used to be the centre for all the estate dealings. It had been closed up and dark. So why not then have had a bit of a cast at the Round if he'd wanted to? Truly it would have been a kind of recovery for him to have been able to do so, is what he had thought. With the memory of that water and the knowledge of the fish, the beautiful salmon, lying there in its depths, moving just slightly, its tail wavering gently in the current and the gills working, in and out, in and out … As though, yes, it really was waiting for him. And, again … *Everything.* Of course it could have been only a recovery indeed, he'd thought, to get down to that particular pool, in the same way as deciding to come back here had been as though making the first steps towards recovering something he'd thought he'd lost, that part of himself that his father had told him he must hold onto in order to feel certain of himself and protected and strong. 'Pull yourself together, Robbie.' Is what his father had always said. Be certain. Be decent. You know the right thing to do, so why not do it? 'What's the matter with you, boy?'

That day, for sure, for the first time in a long time, he'd had these thoughts starting to come into his mind, and more. About the past and not knowing, actually, the right thing to do, not knowing at all. Only knowing instead the many ways you could make yourself sick, over the years, if you took the easy way out, and did so, and over and over again. And what that did to you, weakness, and what he'd made of his life, of its pleasures, yes, but mainly of the things he had done. How he'd allowed himself to become the man who would act the way he had. Mainly that. The choices he'd made, and the sort of people he'd known, the business dealings and the money and the family that he'd lost … All that. That he'd ended up being someone who had forgotten about what it could be like here, with the murmuring comfort of the river and land around to hold him, and had nearly forgotten too about who he had been once, that boy whose father had taught him, as Johnny had, about this place and how it could keep you safe. He'd been thinking about all this and more as he'd started walking the three miles or so along the estate road, walking in a kind of dream, further and further, the car left long behind him by then, to where there'd been yet another huge gate, and this time barbed wire had been wrapped right around the gatepost and across the top of it, and wound through the gate also another kind of wire. The notice there had said simply 'Warning'—as though even if one had been able to get open the great industrial-sized weight of the thing and go through it anyone would have wanted to.

But how he had wanted to. To get to the part just beyond the gate to where there had always been a lovely turn of the river and the start of all the fishing places there that Johnny had shown him, and his father, those two men who had seemed so large to him as a boy. Even as a young man they'd seemed the same. The presence of them, somehow, tall and certain in their ways, and quiet … and yet, there. He hadn't given either of them a second thought for years. Not really. But he was out in the wide air that day, the sun on his back, and he'd been thinking about them then, sure enough, now that he was getting close to the one pool he'd always loved, set so low down in the bank that you couldn't see it from the road, yet knowing once you were down there that the lodge was also just up ahead and you'd be back to it afterwards, Sarah at the door, and there'd be a hot bath and a fire, and they'd all be waiting for him then. Remember? Oh yes, waiting. As though relying upon him, was how it had always felt. Because he'd had to give answers to the questions they'd have ready for him, the right answers, to respond in the way they wanted, speak back to them in the way they expected. Yes, that is how it had been.

So, 'Where have you been, Robbie boy?' Waiting, asking. Sarah. His uncles, cousins. Johnny. His father. And he'd had to reply. To stand up to them, to be a man. 'Where were you?' Johnny asking, and his father. 'What did you see?' Though he'd been shy coming in on them, and uncertain … Still, 'How was your luck this time?' they'd be asking, looking closely at him, as though right inside him. 'You were able?'

For he'd had luck at the Round, had he not? And, yes, it's true, he'd hoped that luck might hold, that he might get to keep it—for back then, in the old days, and maybe later, too. If he'd done everything he was supposed to have done, and done it properly, done it right, 'Then your luck might just stay with you. It might.' Is what Johnny had said to him once. And Johnny the one who knew everything there was to know about this water. From the first time when he'd come here as a boy and met the keeper then and had caught with that man's help his first great fish … Of course Johnny would know how it might be. His, 'How did you get on, then, eh?' His looking him up and down. Oh yes, he remembered alright; Johnny checking up on him, questioning him, 'How?' All of them asking by then, expecting, wanting, judging … that feeling, of them all waiting on him, as though expecting something of him, was how it had felt, demanding that he might have been able to give it, the way they'd be always asking him, back then, in the old days, 'So how was it there, down at the Round?' His father and Johnny and Sarah, and his uncles and aunts and his cousins … gathered together as they were every year at this same place, waiting for him to come in to them with stories of what had happened down at the pool where he'd had so much luck once, and he'd thought, hadn't he, at one point in his life, that his luck might indeed have stayed somehow? His answers to them hold?

No wonder it had always been his favourite part of the water then, and that he'd needed to get to it that day, to the same pool where there had always been so many fish, the deep part where he'd caught his first salmon, and the power of that. How it had seemed to give him something that he'd known otherwise he never could have had. So of course, he'd beaten down the wire at the base of the fence by the last terrible gate with his boot and had managed to scramble under, taking most of the tear from the wire on his jacket, because who cared? When he'd been attending by then only to the memory of that great fish at the end of his line, that first astonishing draw of something down there in the water and the way his father and Johnny had taught him, so gently, to bring it in. 'Easy, now … You're being too hard on him. Easy …' Their voices, as he'd walked along on the soft grass and heather, as though sounding in the air there beside him. 'Gently,' they'd said. 'Be gentle with him …' As he'd played the beautiful fish and brought it in as the men had shown him, this live thrashing lovely thing brought out into the light, pulling and thrusting, and playing it, yes, to catch it, but letting it be killed cleanly too and easily at the end and laid out there on the heather that they had been able to admire its full strength and beauty. 'A bar of silver,' was the way his father had always described the salmon. 'How lucky we are, Robbie.' To have this part of the country to come to. To be inside it, right inside as they had seemed to be back then, kept safe within its waters and land. His father had told him from the start, had he not? 'This place can restore you.'

And yes, no doubt, as he'd been walking the last quarter mile or so across the soft grass and heather to get down to the Round he'd realised that it must have been in his mind for a long time that at some point in his life he would have needed to return to the part of the river where he could remember his father's voice and have the memory of his father's and of Johnny's pride in him, their delight in the way he had taken the salmon that day long ago and had learned to take them afterwards, so cleanly and so well. 'Look at that,' he had heard the men say that day, all that time ago, and days after the first time, and for a few years even. As though he might have heard them talk that way about him still. 'Our boy has done alright after all.'

For how he had needed it, that memory of his father's pride, to get better again. And how it had been as though all the richness and hope he'd had back then in that bright past, for himself and for what his future might be, had been gathered up in his remembering of the great fish laid out beside the deep round pool of water. And how he had needed to believe, too, that day, that he really might have managed it somehow, by being back there again, to recover that part of himself he'd thought he'd lost. As he had had it in mind that it was to have been the beginning of many such returnings, had he not? Had that not also been clearly with him as companion, as the river used to be his companion, that thought? As he'd turned off the soft grass and started down the steep hill towards the Round Pool, thinking even with the razor wire at his back about how it would have been to put a fly out across the water and see what might have happened? How all that he'd loved in his life had been somehow attached to that thought, to that line, to that part of the water?

But as he would remember, years later, and after everything that had made up his life was as though it had never taken place, as though his life itself had never been in his possession, he'd had no rod with him that day. No satchel with flies and line. No kit. He'd been driving, and then he'd been no longer able to drive and had walked, a long walk—and the rest had all just been hopes or imaginings or something else again to do with belief or faith, but not known to him as fact or by experience or truth. Because even without the signs, the gates, the sad loss of the place with no one taking care of it, the minute he'd come to the side of the bank overlooking the Round Pool and got down to where it had been, scrambling through the bracken to the edge of the bit of water that was left there, then he knew how he'd been fooling himself to think anything about coming back here would make it different for him or change him. Because of course he had not been able to bear it, what he'd seen. Though for a split second, for a fraction of a second, even, he'd thought the fish was alive. It had been moving—and yet how? Left on a rock? And with no river? But there it had been, and at first, yes, he had thought it was a beautiful salmon that had been laid out there, freshly caught, its mouth and gills working as though it had just that minute been brought in and landed. He'd started towards it in excitement. But stopped. Because that was no salmon. For a second he hadn't been sure—for there was the colour, the size ... but no. The colour was too bright. And the tail ... it was wrong too. A kind of growth was coming out of it, like a string of weed, and there were no fins, and the eyes were in the wrong place ... the thing was barely a fish at all. It had been moving and writhing, maybe, its mouth opening and closing, the gills working in and out still trying to breathe ... but that was only the activity of all the lice and grubs that were inside it, eating it out from inside, that had made it seem, for just a second or two, as though it were still alive. The disgust had risen up in him then. He'd had to turn away as quickly as he'd seen it. And then to get away, was all he'd wanted then. To be gone from the place and get away from it as quickly as he could, as far away as possible. To get it out of his mind, the sight and the smell and look of it, clawing and scrambling up the side of the riverbank to get back up to the road and from there to the car and then to be gone.

For yes, how he had been frightened. And how, very quickly, he had wanted to be away from it, what he had seen, where he had been that day, not to be anywhere near. Only to run. In the same way as when he'd been a boy he'd wanted to run from anything that frightened him, his father's words, his father's keeper's judgement … always running. Falling and flailing in his rush to get away as fast as he could from anything he feared, only to be gone all he'd wanted, then and always. To forget about any of it, any of the reasons he'd ever had to return, that might have given him pause, a chance to think again about his life and even imagine for a second it could have been different … only to run and run and run. Frightened again as he'd been all his life frightened and always would be, as he'd been frightened of his father and of Johnny, and of his father's sisters and brothers, and of Sarah and everyone and most of all by now frightened of himself, who he had become.

Which he must have known about all along. How far the damage to himself, as much as to the poor place he'd once loved, had eaten in. Though it had only come together as a reaction fully formed in him, the knowledge of the fresh fine depth of the pool drained to bare bones of rock and scree and the dead ugly thing there beside it, in the seconds, minutes, when he'd actually got down and had seen for himself what had become of his beautiful fish and its dark water. Just as the barbed wire and red printed signs may as well have been announcing it from the beginning, 'Warning!' that the ugly thing would be there waiting for him, as it had always been, as it always would be.

And no recovery to be made from that. Though he might let himself think about it sometimes, years later, sitting in his chair. Of how he had gone down to the pool that day believing that there was something in his past he might have found there that he could hold onto, to draw from, to use. To feel better about himself, to feel natural and decent and whole … he might. The image held still in his poor mind of a deep clear place full of mystery and life and that somewhere in its depths there would be resting the great silver bar of a perfect fish, breathing, waiting, fully alive.

Mam's Tables

Funny how things leap out. You're not thinking about them, or about that part of your life at all. You're not dwelling. You're just living, one day, another day and then—Bang. Some scene or other rises up like the crack of a rifle and there's the rabbit killed. Remembering all at once the past you thought was put behind you, being a kid and frightened half the time. Is what comes back to me. The whole mess of it—institutions, foster homes. The going from one place to another, trying this thing, the next—but then, oh look, there was this one house, wasn't there? And the woman in it ... she seemed more than the rest of them to be like a real mother. Is what I'm getting at, and remember good and proper. Because, most of the places, the people ... Well. You let yourself forget.

But Mam was a bit crazy, and not trying to act like she wanted you to need her—is what made her different I guess. All of us thought she was pretty special. She gave us the look, you know: You're my darling only, and she had this word for us, that we were her shakies, all shipmates on some adventure or other. 'Come here, me old shakies,' she'd call out and we'd answer back, 'Ah no, get off! Get out!', but still, we wanted to be close, and she knew we did. It was our routine. There'd be six or seven of us living with her, but she had the time for each of us in turn, as though we really were the only one. 'Come here, you,' she'd be saying, after cooking or washing up or whatever, and we kids would come right back at her that we didn't want to go and sit on her knee for a bit of quiet time and a chat but of course we did want to. We were young, I suppose, and not that tough. Little kids and pretty shaky alright, so Mam's routines and her way of saying things … You don't forget that stuff. Years have gone by, and you've put it away, so you won't think about it, maybe, but even so. It jumps out.

That part of me, though, as I say—my life then and all the rest of it—is not who I am, I like to think. I've kids of my own by now, Donna's from her first marriage, and she knows, my partner knows, where it's at—calm as you like. We've been together seven years come this December, and steady, steady … a full ship on the sea, that's Donna and me, and her never sliding this way or that. She's an only and her parents are still alive. She's got that, Donna has. We'll go round there this Christmas like we're always going around, the whole family out under the macrocarpas on Christmas day and more food than you can imagine, all of us having a laugh. Because Donna's parents … well, even now you can just tell she's still their special little girl.

And, sure, you might say there was something of that sort going on for the kids at Mam's place all those years ago. You might. Six or seven of us but her house was big enough, and the foster people allowed it. That when someone moved on, or found a place back with their own family, the door would be opened up for the next in line. I can admit I liked it there. This was back before property took off and places like hers well out of town were ten a penny and great for any kid. All that space around those kinds of houses then, before the developers got in with their subdivisions. There were the big gardens and the paddocks and what have you, like a world. That whole part of the country left to itself, you might say, and so much of it with the National Park outside your door and the mountain up ahead, all the sky. Of course I'd never want to go back to a city again.

So, yes, it was an easy set-up, and Mam was easy with us, is all there should have been to it. The way she made it seem as though we really were in a gang together, that we were her special crew. It was a pretty good way for a kid to live. She was generous about things getting wrecked and taught us about gardening, flowers. She had loads of cats. You could stay in the bath as long as you wanted, keep the bedside light on through the night if you needed it. And there were books, all kinds, and she never said, oh, this one, or no, not that one. You could just read, whatever. Or watch telly. She didn't mind about the stuff of rules, behaviour. And she was a great cook, always talking with us about what she was making and what we were going to have. Roasts and chips and pies and all kinds of puddings. She was easy with us that way as well, never making us eat what we didn't like, only her own recipes, everything we wanted on our plate. That house of hers was mainly kitchen. Upstairs were bedrooms, the bathrooms—but her own room on the ground floor had once been a sitting room, maybe, so the whole place was set up as though it was for all of us, as though Mam had made it that way, as though she really had. And to be in that big old kitchen of hers with its book-shelves and the cooker that had a fire in it, sitting around, all of us, at this one enormous table ... it felt safe. It did. Her, 'Come here, you' and our answer, 'Ah, get off' but knowing she would gather us in even so, to be there at the table with her, to be close. We'd be hanging around, always hungry, wanting this and that, and Mam might be over there at the bench, cutting something up or mixing ingredients in a bowl, plums on the stove, or sugar carrots, some kind of preserve, whatever. She might be looking out the window talking back to us, the radio on. That room was where everything happened. And the table, that table of Mam's in the middle of it all ... it was like a raft. It was like living your life there.

At teatime we'd all be sitting down together at that table, and there was room enough, you could always move over and let someone else in. It seemed some kids were always there. One boy, much older than me, was forever drawing. Pictures of buildings, the insides of them. Churches. His papers were all piled up at one end and we didn't have to clear them away. The girls over on the other side of him would be painting their nails and going through magazines: I like her, No I don't like her. There'd be talking or not talking. Homework, doing that. Or not being able. You could do whatever you wanted. There was this girl I quite liked who wrote tiny poems on pieces of cardboard and made them into little boxes, and she'd be there, colouring and gluing, writing away. Mam didn't make anyone stop whatever it was they were up to when it was time to eat, but we all did stop. Because she sat down then and we really were like her family, gathered around. Her saying to us, 'Ok, here we all are, me old shakies', and, 'Isn't this nice?' Like saying grace, kind of. Like my in-laws do. Only not the same because … I trusted the table. Even now, I find myself thinking about it, though I know I can't trust it, and that none of this is really a sure memory of anything that went on for me back then, when I was a kid. Still, it was nice, like Mam said it was. To be there, sitting there. I thought so. Everyone came and went at that house, we kids came and went, and though I never really developed the habit, you might say, of intimacy, that old woman seemed to have made something that would hold us and that would last. Her saying, 'Let's have a good look at you, eh?' amid all the coming and going and getting you up on her knee for a chat. I can remember exactly the feel of the big arms, the bony leg under the cotton dress, winter or summer, the man's cardigan she wore if it was cold and me sitting up there against its dark wool. Making things seem so … Yeah. Nice. It was another of her words, in that phrase, 'Isn't this nice?' She would be speaking as though to herself, 'What are we going to do with you, eh, you old shaky-quake?' and she would put her fingers through my long hair and draw patterns into it, braiding, and with a soft brush making a style, even. 'You going to calm down and relax or what?' she'd say to me. 'There's nothing to worry about. Nothing at all.' No wonder, no wonder, stupid, I thought I was part of her gang. We all did. I was allowed to wear trousers and have my shirt off all through the summer and Mam would still call me pretty. 'You're a special girl, Shirley,' she used to say. 'Don't let anyone talk you out of it.'

But talk does talk, and that means it shifts and it changes. Mam's own words did.

Bang, remember? A heart put out? Well that's what happened there, alright. Because for sure and I know it, I have it in my history, those same sentences of Mam's that let me in and held me close were also how everything got mucked up for me there, at that house— and I'll never tell Donna, I won't, about how that changed things for me. I couldn't describe it. How, even though back then I might have liked to think otherwise—that there was a steady platform, a good floor to stand a table on—I know a great hole is there, in that kitchen, in Mam's old red lino. It's like a bulldozer's come in. So there might have been all that braiding, and that 'you're special'. Special, nothing. You need to be able to hold onto what people say if their words are going to be of any use to you and be something real. Descriptions of a life have to stay the same, see, or else they fall away—and I don't have the first clue, me, about who I am, who I might be. Though I've tried to fix things, and some might say I do, making it up so nice with Donna and the kids and a job and all the rest of it, still I've learned not to trust words to have much in the way of truth about them. And I won't tell Donna, I won't. That just when I think I'm getting over any kind of remembering, the past jumps out and I'm back in Mam's kitchen again, falling straight through the floor of that same red lino, into the dark.

When that happens … well. I leave Donna's house then, I do. You might think I could avoid it, that I'd be busy enough not to want to be bothered but the hole opens up under my feet when I least expect it and I have to leave where I live then. I have to just leave it behind. With all kinds of thoughts coming trailing behind me—that I don't owe Donna anything, that they're her kids not mine … All of that kind of evil thinking pulling me away from everything I've built up, the life I've made with others who I care about. I just go off. I get in the car—and this could be any day or hour, before work, maybe, or in the middle of the day, once just after midnight and they were all out at a party … I just get in the car, and I'm gone. I drive all the way up north, through that same old National Park, to arrive some-where that's, I guess, 'in the vicinity' as they might say in the cop shows. In that 'neck of the woods' for sure. Because though I never make driving round to find Mam's old place part of the story, oh, I'm in the area, alright, I'm nearby. I book myself into some motel or other. I lock the door. I take stuff with me to make me sleep and I stay in bed then, for all the time I'm there. I stay in that place with the blinds closed and the door locked until I'm ready to come home.

And is it fear of being left behind or leaving that I've got? Frightened to be there, in that dark room, or of the house where I've come from? Frightened to be where my life is now, or back where it used to be? The motel means both, I reckon. That 'You're special, Shirley' ringing in my ears by now. Because … special. That's just another word, something anyone might say as easy as lie. Like Mam's, 'Come here, shaky …' and being her shipmates and up on her knee for a talk and a cuddle. That whole story, it was none of it true. We were shaky alright, she got that part right, at least. A bunch of kids with no homes of their own, and forever coming, going.

Shaky not the half of it, I might say—but still that old woman had us believing in what we had there, with her dinners and her tables, all her talk. Even now I find myself wanting to believe in it, even now. The sun coming in through the kitchen door when we sat down in summer, a fire in the autumn and winter and the lights on. Because who wouldn't want to have that? To have it be part of who you are? Who wouldn't?

But Mam had a kid of her own was what none of us ever knew—not until afterwards, I mean. It turned out she'd grown up years ago, this girl had, and moved far away and didn't see anything of her mother— those reasons not my concern. Because why she wouldn't want to return, or why her mother would never mention her own child … I can't guess at it. I can't care. Only that the old woman ended up hearing the full story, oh she heard alright, that her daughter had been sick and she'd been sick for ages, for months in one of the big hospitals down south, coming out for a bit but then having to go back in there. And all the time, through all of it, the operations and doctors and the treatments and the rest, she had never contacted her mother once, or told her anything. Someone had to come to the door, someone who knew her or knew someone who did, to tell her mother what had happened, some stranger, to tell a mother something she was never expecting. And sure, of course I can understand how that must have hit hard. Getting that kind of news and from some person you've never seen before … it hits hard. Mam told us that, afterwards—trying to explain, I suppose, to make us feel better, saying she was sorry for how she'd been—but by then it was too late. The table had been overturned, so to speak, and I, for one, wouldn't sit down with her there again. I left her house quite soon after. I started acting up again, like I'd been before, all my old tricks. I made it impossible for me to stay. Because the hole in the floor … it gapes.

And down into the bloody dark you go.

So it was that one minute an old woman's got a houseful of other people's kids sitting in her kitchen having their tea, having a great old time actually and imagining they could live this way forever, and the next it's all over. Is the way life is, I reckon, and once the remembering has started up I'm back there reliving that one stupid night as though it might be the worst thing in my life and God knows it's not the worst. But there it is, the scene of it, and playing out like a story that's as unreliable as I am, the front doorbell going and Mam—and here I am still calling her that, 'Mam' like she's our mother, like she's someone we might respect—she gets up from where she's been sitting, 'our Mam', and she's gone for a while. The rest of us are just carrying on, talking and having a laugh, having a bit of fun the way we always did, with jokes and all the rest of it and afterwards there'd be pudding and then clearing the plates away and getting out the chess or Monopoly or some of us were doing a bit of knitting, someone else saying, 'put the kettle on, will you, where are the biscuits …' Only the front door was a door no one ever used and she was gone for a while, our Mam was, so we should have known, shouldn't we, while we were carrying on, making such a racket ourselves we couldn't hear anything, be aware of anything, that something was up?

But we were just all of us on the raft of the table. And it seemed, for so long it seemed, as if nothing had happened to change that. Only the raft holding us, keeping us … as though it always would. It was a summer's night, and nothing did seem to happen, did it? In my mind nothing did, and we are still safe, all of us, and on the raft and we will stay here together, a real family, you see, no time pressing in to take that away. Only to stay, stay in that moment, with all the other kids at Mam's house and nothing happening around us to change it … Nothing … Until—after how long? It was a summer evening, remember, so hard to tell, light seemed to fill the room as though it would never leave but of course it would leave—Mam came back into the kitchen, she sat down at the table, and we must have stopped then, what we were doing, what we were talking about, we stopped. We did. We looked at her, like—what now? What's happening? Only instead of her looking back at us, her gang there all together so she could call out to us and we could answer, instead of any of our routine, of her asking what it was that we might want or we might do now, or could think of or imagine, or what of anything, me darling shakies, might you need? What might you need? Instead of any of it she was quiet. She didn't say a word. She didn't even seem to notice we were there.

I remember the mighty stillness of it, that silence—none of her usual words to fill it, none of the things she would call out to us or ask or say that we would answer, 'Ah, get off! Get out!' Only silence. Like the motel. That stop of time. That dark. A silence that lasted for—maybe a moment. Or a second. Or some moments. Hours. A lifetime. I don't know. And then someone said—I said?—'Mam?' And she turned, this woman, this mother who'd been looking after us for so long, who'd fed us and talked with us and had the time in her day for each of us, you know, each kid, and we loved her, we did, we loved her, she turned to face me, and slowly is how it seems, like coming into focus, looking at me but not saying, 'Come here' or, 'What are we going to do with you, eh, Shirley?' Only instead looking at me as though she couldn't understand why I would even speak to her, as though she didn't know me at all. What I was doing there, sitting at her table, who was I, anyhow? And then she started looking around at all of us in turn, one after the other, as though she didn't know who any of us were, any of us, this bunch of kids sitting at her table, who were we? Eh? Who? That was when all the safety of it, the table, the way it held us together, was gone. Only silence, the floor opening up. The gaping hole. And that anything could have been depended on back there in that part of your strange life or now … Where the hell did that kind of thinking ever come from, eh old shaky? You belong in a motel, alright, with the door closed tight, sweetheart, if you think for a moment anything you might have or had once could be relied upon or needed. That a few words someone might say would be the whole story, that a sentence or two could have the power to make you feel safe and fixed in this world … You reckon you might have acquired that habit? To think the table was secure? That raft? Then you're some kind of mucked-up old fool you old shaky, alright. Words change, and you should know it. Words for comfort, words for joy … they shift and slide and they crack and go off like a gun. Turn into something else altogether and it doesn't matter what you say afterwards to make up for it, to try and take back what you've said. Words change the way the world is, and they can do it in a heartbeat. You only have to open your mouth and speak.

'Listen, you kids, all of you,' Mam said that night, after the silence, after the stop of time in which everything that had gone on before was rearranged, and I would come to stop believing in the safety of anything that was said. 'Get out,' she said. She the one saying that to us, not us to her. Not, 'Come here, you' and us answering, 'Ah, no, get off! Get out!' This time she was the one telling us, 'Get out.' Everything was changed. 'I can't bear the sight of any of you,' she said then, and she picked up her plate and she threw it across the room. Then she reached over with one arm and swept all the stuff off the table straight onto the floor, the bread and the food and our water and her wine. 'All this muck. All of you …' she said. 'Out. I want you out.' Her daughter was dead and now everything was broken. 'Come here' could never return, to gather around. The plates were everywhere and smashed, and food and mess was all over the floor, but it was the words she'd spoken that were like a mighty storm that had overturned us, the glasses and forks and knives tossed on the sea as we ourselves were tossed and fallen and how do you climb back on again when the thing you'd been on is gone under? You don't. You don't climb on.

And so I have come to write about it here, of what happened to me at that woman's house, how she spoke and how her speaking changed, and the bludgeoning of that, the damage—but I won't tell the story to anyone, I won't speak it out loud. How words told us kids that night, and in seconds, what we had until then not let ourselves know or else had made ourselves forget. That we weren't ever part of Mam's family, that all of it, the meals and the kitchen and everything lovely that went on in that woman's house, for any of the children who ended up there, still none of it was any kind of real description. That night it was chicken stew with apricots. Sweetcorn. Gravy. It was the best kind of sticky yams and potatoes and dark sauce, and after, Mam had told us before, there'd be chocolate tart and ice cream, and a new board game she'd just bought for us to play … but those details, sentences, acts of care held close in their nouns and adjectives and their verbs … how surely, easily they get turned into nothing. Everything turning into nothing, then, and you don't want to talk about that to anyone. You never will.

And of course I understand, I've thought it through. I'm smart enough. We weren't hers. We were foster kids. And her own child was dead. I get that. How it must have made her crazy as it would make anyone crazy, learning the way she did that night from a stranger and all at once about what had happened to her girl. Of course I have empathy for that situation, I do, and can understand why it might have been the way it was. But it leaps out, what went on that one night, continuing to interfere with the way I see things, do things, believe. Reminding me that it's words, words, words that describe what you are in this world, old shaky. They sound in the air. They create a direct hit. The table gets tipped and all the lovely things on it, they're on the floor.

Poor Beasts

'You couldn't make it up,' says Aly.

He's sitting at the table in our kitchen, looking out over the hills.

'It's like a short story,' I reply. 'Only if I write it as one, I'll have to change the names of the estate, the people. You, even. We couldn't, you know, let it get around. How you feel about the changes they are making. You'd be out of a job.'

'I'm out of a job anyway,' says Aly. 'I reckon. But, yeah. I see what you mean.'

He takes a sip of his coffee. Spends a long time settling the mug back down on his plate, just so, beside the scone sitting there he's barely touched. I've known him and his wife for thirty years. More than thirty. They've looked after the Ben Mhorlaich estate for most of that time. His wife, Margaret, is one of the most practical and far-sighted people I know. If there's something I want to find out about—from pruning an apple tree to making a time-and-place line of all the characters in *War and Peace*, Margaret is the one who can tell me.

Right now, I wish she was here to comfort me about this news Aly's just served. While I was getting the scones out of the oven—a particular sort of scone I make—he told me then, while my back was to him and I couldn't react straight away with holding the hot tray, and then dealing with them, taking them off and getting them onto a cooling rack.

Only to say, 'What?' and 'I don't believe it ...' while I was putting them onto a plate and getting out the butter and cheese. Normally Aly loves these scones. I put herbs and olives in them. Today it was one bite, and that was it. I didn't feel like eating either.

'It is like a short story,' I say again and break off a lump of olive and fiddle with the crumbs around it onto the plate. 'It has all the elements. A lovely place, a way of living that seems unchanging, and then in one summer ...'

'Margaret says it's the end of the lodge,' says Aly quietly, as though to himself. 'She says they'll sell all the shooting to the Chinese or the Russians, whoever pays the most, and they'll just bring in their own parties from one of the fancy hotels—that one near Rose Hall, say—for the day.'

'But—'

'And a great crowd of four-wheel drives all over the hill,' Aly finishes. As I say, that's what these big outfits use in the Highlands now. Dozens of them. So they can come in, get out ...'

'Like a war,' I say.

'Some kind of awful thing, for sure,' Aly says. He goes to pick up his mug again, but then doesn't. 'I don't know what to think about it ...' His voice trails off.

I can't bear it. I stand and go over to the window. It's early spring and the hills are greening. Under all the brown and grey and stone, it's there, the beginnings of the summer ahead and all the light. This morning, very early, before the rest of them were up, I was awake. I stood at the kitchen window then and watched the sun rise from behind the hills, everything brightening, second by second, a kind of photo coming into print, bleaching out all of the dark and gradually showing outlines, shapes. As I stood and watched, a herd of deer came running like water down off the side of the furthest hill, like a run of water, yes, then taking form as individual animals as they got closer. Closer they came, and closer, the entire herd on the move as though something were after them, driving them onwards. Down they came, making for the far field that used to be for the MacKays' sheep and is now all empty pasture, coming through that and across the river, over the high water like it was nothing, and then straight up towards the house, towards our house—me … where I was standing as though waiting for them. For a second it really did seem like that. As though the deer were going to run straight through the walls of the house and into the kitchen and all around me in one great rush of movement, onwards, forwards, the house as invisible to them as the river had been, coming right up to just before the fenceline at the bottom of the garden before they veered off to the left, into the little wood that runs up by the farm road, disappeared into it and were gone.

The rest of them had been still in their beds, my daughters, home from university with friends, and my husband, and my two cousins who were staying with us from Canada, a houseful of us—and all of them asleep—yet I'd seen this thing. I'd had this moment in my life when I'd thought, been overwhelmed by the feeling, that we could have all been surrounded by the deer that had been rushing across the land, that they might have run right through the house and out again. In the few seconds of my watching there had been no break in their stride.

'It doesn't bear thinking about,' says Aly now. 'I'll take some more of that coffee, Beth, since you've made it.'

I turn, reach for the pot on the bench beside me, and in that second of turning feel how old I am, how old we both are, Aly and

I, two old friends sitting here. Though we may be going about the place as always, and I am riding as well as I ever have, and doing everything as fast, and still up and down to Edinburgh and London every few weeks or so with Robbie to see the girls and not even noticing it … still. In that little old lady gesture of my turning I feel every one of my years built up within me, thirty years in this dear, dear place.

I fill Aly's cup, top up my own.

'They can't afford the taxes now,' he says, 'is just about the sum of it. Margaret and I have seen this coming. And now this guy, Povlsen. Buying up every estate in Sutherland and Caithness he can get his hands on, one by one like he's playing Monopoly and the Scottish Government are helping him. Nothing good can come from that either.' He takes up a scone, puts it down. 'We've been out of a job for a while, you could say, Margaret and I. And all of us. There'll be no more gamekeepers anywhere in Sutherland with the way things are going. But, after that meeting yesterday, the way it is there, in the Estate Office … well …'

'It doesn't bear thinking about,' I repeat after him, using his own sentence, filling up his coffee again like someone with no mind or heart or will. Because how can I have will or heart or mind to hear what I am hearing though it's not for the first time. Margaret and Aly, Robbie and I … we've talked about these things before, seen all the changes that are afoot, the legislation that's going on with everything being put in place and none of us even aware of it most of the time, but still a deep feeling, gone deep in, that the land is gathering a different meaning to itself … especially here, where we are, though there's no one much who'll talk about it, how the big estates are selling off one by one and not as going concerns, as it would have been in the old days, but for different reasons—wind turbines, fish farms, whatever will pay. That meeting Aly had yesterday … that says a lot. That there are these meetings, and involving lawyers now, not anyone he knows, and with the old factor long gone. It was some guy from one of the government departments doing all the talking this time, Aly said. 'Centralised initiatives'—that was how he put it, and lodges closed up the length of Sutherland and even the shooting, the bit of fishing, not like it was once, but all day trippers coming up from London and going back the same night, bringing their own guns with them and God knows how they behave, out on the hill, these people who've bought up vast acreages in a place they know nothing about, and don't care to know except that it is there on their lists of assets.

'It's not the first time, though,' I say to Aly out loud, thinking about all of this. Three years ago he was in my kitchen telling me about a new manager brought in from Edinburgh who had been up seeing all the gamekeepers in the region, telling them their time was marked. It would be Knight Frank and Bell Ingrams doing all the estate managing from now on, he said, no need to keep couples on in full-time work in these remote places. Things seemed to go quiet then, after that visit. But things never go completely quiet. Once change comes, change moves things on, and in the parts where it goes quiet it's just us, the people who live here, getting used to change, is all, that's it there in the back of our minds and so we come to expect it. Still, 'We have heard all this before,' I say, to comfort Aly, to comfort myself. 'We have seen all this coming.' For months, yes. Longer. Aly and Margaret have known their time at Ben Mhorlaich was numbered to months, there were no longer years in it. The factor who was no longer the factor, a Bell Ingrams agent, called a meeting with them, not long after the September Referendum. The estates all over Scotland were bringing in lawyers by then, 'to assess the situation' was the phrase Aly told me the Ben Mhorlaich people had used. Not all of them would be affected, of course, but with forthcoming changes due to new land legislation, and with—as Aly had looked into all this—'the behind-the-scenes dismantling of powers' as it was described, in their bureaucratic jargon, of 'certain landholdings, contexts, situations' some of the larger estates were going to have to divest themselves of properties 'damn smartly' he had told him, this guy, Aly said, as though it was a fun thing, a wanted thing.

But it was only now, I am thinking, at this meeting yesterday … it was only yesterday that the estate actually informed their employees, only then that they told them, formally, told Aly and Margaret Sutherland, told them outright that they'd need to start looking for accommodation and alternative employment for the 'forthcoming period'—another phrase taken out of the paperwork, Aly said.

'They tell me they can find something for me to do over this winter,' he says now, draining his coffee. 'But I've had enough.' He lets out a short, bitter laugh. 'We're going back to Perthshire. An old friend has some fencing work he can give me, and some other bits and pieces. Margaret's sister is in Loch Tummell. We'll manage.'

All the time, during this grim talk, I am there doing nothing, saying nothing—just hearing his words and saying them back to myself, in my mind, arranging the things on the table, moving them from here back to there, like pieces on a chessboard: sugar, mugs. My dumb scones. Everything silent, actually. No life in anything at all. Despite Aly talking, the things he says, there are no words, really, for any of this. No expression for the weight of it, feeling the awful knowledge of time and what is ahead. Then, thinking about that, the hopelessness of it, there in my mind appear the deer again, running down off the hills as they had been early in the morning, streaming down towards me in the kitchen as though I wasn't even there.

'But I can't think of this part of the world without you two in it,' I say then.

With the deer running, I can see them coursing down the hill.

'Margaret and I …' I say. 'We've been talking about the situation for some time … but even so—'

The deer running still, streaming down the hill like water.

'Is there nothing we can do?'

The whole thing, the sight of them, had been over in seconds.

'Seems, Beth, nothing,' says Aly, standing up now to go. 'You'll see Margaret later,' he adds, leaning down to give me a hug goodbye. 'Say good morning to that lazy family of yours,' he says. 'Where are they anyhow?'

'Robbie's taken them to Dornoch,' I say. 'My sister wanted a run with him to see that new shop with all the tweed and the pottery, and my cousins have gone with them for the ride. The kids are around somewhere, though they may have gone too, a couple of them …'

'And I thought they were all sleeping,' Aly says. 'Well there you go.'

He's on his way to the door and I'm behind him. He ducks as he always has to, at the entrance to the porch. 'Margaret will call in around five, she said. She's got some cuttings for you. They might see her—your lot—in Dornoch.'

'Might,' I say. 'No, they weren't sleeping.' No, none of us were. Yet look at us all, it occurs to me, we may as well be. Sleeping and sleepwalking through all of this change as it collects around us, inevitable as the kind of weed you see in the Loch up behind the hills now, bright green and strong, changing the colour of the water as you look at it, bright and strange and artificial, and killing the fish, killing everything as it grows.

'We may as well all be asleep …' I say then. But Aly doesn't hear me. He is walking down the garden towards his truck parked out on the road. I feel like I am in a dream … a dream, only I am asleep in it. Asleep while the deer come down. Asleep while the land they come through is sold off, piece by piece—to Russia, China, this man Povlsen … whoever pays most, fastest. I walk with Aly to the gate, unspeaking. Dumb and meek, with nothing to say, like one of his dogs who I guess soon he'll have to shoot or rehome because sure enough he can't take a kennel full of gun dogs and hounds to Margaret's sister's in Tummell. And over everything a feeling of heaviness, impending change and endings that have their beginnings in things that have been going on for a while now, I can see it, like a dreamer. First with the turbines and you couldn't go anywhere in Sutherland or Caithness without seeing them—what was it Robbie and I found out—that Sutherland had been designated a 'red zone' for wind power development? So-called 'renewables' as though the people who live here might get renewed energy, cheap and free as the wind when all we get are the monstrous white machines every-where you look and the same high energy bills and the massive lorries carving up roads all over the places where we live and sinking aggre-gate into the peat in order that those huge towers have somewhere to stand, so the rivers are flooding now, every spring and the bright weed starts growing in the high lochs from the drain-off … Bright, bright change, all of it, across the ancient hills …

'Do you know what Margaret says?' Aly had told me, just before this story begins. 'She says it's the poor beasts she pities. With no one there to manage things, to make sure they're properly looked after on the hill, then taken out, properly, you know, with a good gun. Stalked properly and so on, things done in the right way …'

'I hadn't even thought—' I'd started then to speak but couldn't. Even then, I'd been fiddling with my stupid baking, fiddling at the oven, at the stove because what could I say? Struck dumb with the image before me of four-wheel drives cutting over the same soft hills where Aly and his father before him had walked, with quiet knowl-edge and history, invisibly tracking the herd, picking out the oldest, the sick, the one with the game leg that would bring it down anyway for a long, slow death away from the others … Walking across the same land upon which I'd seen the animals coming through this morning, their easy, momentary flight … now four-wheel drives and firing rifles out of open windows. No one knowing what they were doing. Aly and Margaret far, far away and the lodge opened up for a week or so every year as a sort of rich man's hotel.

'Helicopters even, some folk use,' Aly had said. 'Just firing down on them, while the deer are running, just random, scatter firing and wounding them, not finishing the job, leaving them there … Christ. You couldn't make it up.'

'I will write about all this, though,' I manage, as he's just about to go. 'There's this land futures book I've been asked to think about …'

Aly swings the door open and starts up the truck. 'Just remember it's not a story, that's all. Look after yourself, Beth,' he says as he starts to reverse into our drive to head back up the way, to Ben Mhorlaich. 'Give my best to the others. Tell Robbie I'll stop by one of these days soon and we'll have that dram.'

Dreede

She watched it as it turned back and seemed to want to pick up the crumb, but then flipped around again, with its strange twisty body doing a sort of miniature jump.

'Miniature.'

Miniature was a word Anna loved.

'I love miniature things,' she'd told her schoolteacher at the end of term. 'I love drawing them, and I love to spell the word.' She'd started to say the letters, writing them with her finger on her hand: 'M then the I—then N—I' before the teacher stopped her. 'Now that's enough Anna. Why not go and play with the other girls, while they're all outside? There's no need to be here in the classroom on your own.' Anna had smoothed down her uniform where it had been crumpled; no, she wasn't going to go.

'You're a strange miniature person,' she whispered to the ant now. 'Mini mini miniature …' Why weren't its friends helping it? All the other animals, those tiny creatures, also miniature, who lived here in the crack in the wall … they weren't being kind. Anna could see that with her own eyes, by the way they were greeting each other, and stopped to touch, this one to that, without really stopping, or finding it frightening. It was only their way of saying hello. 'Hello.' And, 'Hello.' 'Hello.'

It was the way people did it, greeted. Stopping and touching. Only this time touching with their feelers as they went on their way.

But yes, this miniature one … Anna could see that her particular friend was different from the rest—from his broken-looking body to the way he was with the crumb. He went to it, the flake of pastry, but couldn't lift it. He was interested but unable to carry.

'Get up,' her mother said, from the lounger. 'Let me put some sun cream on your shoulders. You'll get burnt, sitting over there where there's no shade.'

Anna didn't need to look over at her to know she was there. 'Burnt!' That word! The kind her mother loved. None of these creatures down here by the wall cared about the sun. They were running around, being extremely busy. Extremely.

'E-X-T-R-E …'

'Get up,' her mother said again.

But no, first Anna had to see, must just observe, how busy the tiny animals were. Here one. Here another. Ever since she'd given them the end of her croissant, sprinkled it into pieces and left it along the ridge of the wall, she'd seen from the start how this had given all of them plenty to do.

But only this broken one who had the strange shape that wasn't like the others—more like he was two ants squashed into one and with a part of his back missing … he was the only fellow not part of the gang. He wasn't picking up the miniature sections of crumb like the rest of them and bearing them away …

'Bearing them away,' she said out loud, a lovely sentence, and with beautiful words that spelled in a certain way to have meanings that were old fashioned and true … For, bearing, bare, borne … how they were bearing the pieces of pastry away and off into the crack in the wall. Only, only … this one particular miniature. He couldn't join in.

Sometimes, Anna saw it, another ant came up to him and touched and for a second it seemed as though he might help, and then another, but then that ant too went away busily with the rest and he was left alone. Yes, the others went about their work so busily—all the rest of them, she'd watched, 'observed'—they'd be running along and touching each other, using their tiny feelers to speak, running out from the crack in a long line straight to the flakes of pastry by her foot, that she kept there, so still, without moving, without moving her 'bare foot' that had the other kind of spelling, a homophone her teacher said it was. A Homo-Phone. She continued to watch. How the ants all did it, how they picked up each piece of crumb onto their backs before going back to where they'd come from, all in the same one long line of going out and coming in. And those loads they carried had been part of her breakfast! Something so ordinary now so extremely, she stopped to spell the word, E-X-T-R-E-M-E-L-Y, interesting.

Ants were animals; insects were. She was a girl. The girl had told her mother what was taking place here by the wall, she'd gone over to talk to her about it earlier, but her mother's eyes had stayed closed. Anna had that whole sentence written, a sort of story, in her mind.

'Mmmm,' her mother had said. 'Whatever, Anna.' She was only a daughter after all. A girl. Anna put her finger out, gently, gently, to the broken one, to its funny little jumping body. So miniature. It stopped. Anna waited but nothing happened. It was as though she might have killed it. It wasn't moving but had become like a dot.

'Did you hear what I said?' her mother's voice came at her through the thick Greek air.

'You need cream on. Come over here.'

Greek air, hot air.

Cream on.

They were in a villa in a place called Kefalonia. K-E-F-A-L-O-N-I-A. A difficult sounding yet easy word. 'It's in Greece,' she'd told her father when he'd asked where her mother was taking her for her holidays.

'I know it's in Greece, you loon,' he'd said, scrabbling the top of her head with his hand the way he always did. He loved words like 'loon', 'noodle', 'crazeeee'. With them came down his hand. 'I'll take you there myself sometime if you'd like that,' he'd said, scrabbling and messing up her hair.

But, 'No.' For there was no point in him saying that. 'I can spell it for you, though …' she'd said.

'Oh, please.' He stopped his awful patting. 'Get outta here …'

She thought now, looking at this little Dreede before her, this Mr Miniature, this little Mr Mini Mini Man, who was scrabbling himself down there on the ground and who she'd decided just this second did indeed have exactly the same interesting sounding name as her father, how handsome her father was. He was. Hand-Some. Other ladies said it. Her mother. And with his American accent, his way of speaking … Loon. Crazeee. 'How she loved, loved, loved her daddy.' She had that somewhere, all written down. Even though he made her head hurt when he touched her hair and she never got to stay more than one night in his house. Still …

'She loved, loved, loved …'

Dreede kicked and turned. When her father touched her like that, rubbing, rubbing at her hair, she acted like she acted all the time, stone still, all still, like she was dead. To be touched was a terrible thing. And look at this tiny one now that she'd taken her finger away: He was acting the same way, maybe? With the piece of pastry and deciding, deciding about it, but being, after the touch of the other ant upon it, so very, very still? Because her father only did that, too, like that other ant had done, put his hand out, to be friendly. To scrabble at the top of her head.

'What?' he always said when she stopped what she was doing, went dead still. Then, often. 'Christ. What's wrong with you?'

Because people didn't know, didn't know, didn't know. What it was like not to want to be touched. Ever. Ever. Her mother behind her, any minute, any second with the tube of cream. Teachers. Other girls at school. Everyone, everyone.

She'd thought Dreede was dead. That's how much he'd hated her enormous finger.

'Don't worry, my friend,' she whispered. 'I won't do that terrible thing again.'

All Gone

She put her hands in deep among the baby things to where the guns were. There, underneath the sleepsuits and the tiny cotton T-shirts and the laundered nappies fresh back from the washing service, she could feel them, the smooth polished barrels of the Sig Sauers, the hook of the trigger on the P238 with its blunt snout and the round opening where the bullets would come out. Everything was in place—the situation of the weapons, the box of ammunition beside them. It was a kind of relief, she said, to touch the various shapes, to be familiar with their contours and outlines, and afterwards she knew she could breathe again. 'That was it exactly,' she told me. 'Just by reminding myself they were there, I became so calm.'

No one else would know that of course. At the arrest, in all the papers ... it never came out, her secret, that tucked up among the clean muslins she would use to wipe Bobby down after he'd sicked up her milk and under piles of Laura's little pyjamas and miniature knickers and Tim's prep school shorts and socks and shirts, a pair of Micro Compacts were ... *nestled*. That was the word she used. The cold metal touch of them after the softness of all the baby stuff giving her such pleasure, she said. Pieces that, in their weight and size, embodied perfectly the melding together of form and function. 'And it's strange, don't you think?' she cast her eyes around for a second, as though looking for the answer to her question, then smiled, her brilliant, lovely smile, and laughed. 'That after all I've gone through, I would still find them now as I did then, attractive, interesting objects, and that using them was going to be—absolutely—something I wanted to do.'

I didn't know where to look, of course. But this story, report or whatever … well, it's not about me. It's about giving a clear picture, a portrait, of the kind of person who would do what she did, who would take her thoughts that far.

'Did you ever think about sending them back?' I asked her at one point, after she'd said straight out that she'd made the purchase for a very definite purpose. 'Did you recognise that the thought you had was dangerous? That it could only finish with an ending of one kind?' I remember she put her head down as though praying, and for a moment I believed I was going to see evidence of some kind of regret, that she would become the fully comprehensible version of the woman she'd always been—responsible, trustworthy, a loyal friend and good neighbour, the attractive wife and mother who had moved here to our street when she was pregnant with her third child, as open-hearted and generous as the next person.

But no. She'd looked at me and yawned, tucked a strand of blonde hair behind her ear. 'It was great,' she simply said. 'I knew when I put the order in to the guy who had the friend with access to the website, that those particular items were going to be my "get out of jail free" card'. She laughed. 'The whole thing,' she emphasised, 'my decision, what I did … one great, exceptional feeling of escaping for good a situation I'd found myself in and wanted no more a part of—believe me, it's all fine.'

The 'guy who had the friend with access to the website' is no one they have been able to trace so far. I've read about these kinds of people, of course, the dark web and all that. I've seen the articles and books that show how it's big business, how everyone is up to something or other; people talk about it now. That you can buy anything online with little in the way of questions asked. And so in this instance: she'd met someone, she said, through a pornography site she used, which she had learned of from one of the mothers in the Thursday morning coffee group for toddlers and babies that she went along to when Tim was at school and Laura in the nursery next door where this whole story, you might say, finds its focus. 'Cause and effect' as she liked to put it. One thing leading to another, and a complex aftermath gathered up by a first thought that had preceded all the others and which rested in turn upon a certain kind of life with its rules and order and expectations that, on the whole, had always been met. Nothing more dramatic than that, see? She was always reminding me. 'Nothing.'

Certainly the transaction itself couldn't have been more straight-forward. She'd simply withdrawn cash in various increments from her own account and deposited it into another she'd been given details of in an anonymous email—quite a bit of the 'slush fund', as she called it, from the week's shopping that was given to her by her husband every Monday. 'Well, a massive amount, actually,' she confided—and that was that. Such a sum was to cover all her domestic needs, and this was 'one of those needs,' she said. It was that kind of marriage. Charles was generous, she added, and the amount had only increased as did his time spent away from her, accelerating from the occasional late night at work, to most nights, to weekends as well, occasionally, along with the 'business trips' and 'vacations with US clients'. She hated all that, but the women she counted as friends said the same about their marriages, she told me. It was just the fact of a certain kind of lifestyle, choices made. 'You make your bed; you lie in it. Ha ha,' they agreed. 'It doesn't need to be a big deal.' And so, perhaps, it didn't. Or she had learned how to stop allowing it to be—with the deep breathing she was learning in her one-to-one chakra realignment sessions really helping, along with treating herself to something special from Bond Street or Harvey Nicks when she needed to. For there were lots of things she 'needed'. A lot of women are like that, I know. And so, in turn, the money went out of her account without a husband even noticing, in the way that none of those husbands of her friends might notice what was being spent and how, into some sort of holding reserve, some financial service somewhere. Then, that payment, too, must have gone through because the package duly arrived in the post on a cold March morning—a special delivery company she didn't recognise—and heavy it was to take from the young man who handed it to her, looking her in the eye. 'You got that?' he asked, when she'd placed it on the hall table to sign the shipping note, and was holding her pen poised above the form he'd clipped to a board for her to sign. He tapped her on the knuckle three times with his long index finger. 'You gotta sign, sweetheart,' pointing to the blank space for her signature, 'here.' And before she'd whisked the box up to the linen cupboard to hide it away there, she did. She signed.

By then the reaction she'd discovered in herself following the incident with the little Pakistani girl at Laura's nursery had become a marked thing. For yes, that was certainly the catalyst, she said, for everything else that followed; where this story, as I wrote before, 'finds its focus'. Because although weeks had passed since that day, she kept finding the smell of the other child, the family, on Laura's hands. In the bath at night she'd scrub her daughter all over, but on her hands especially, using a brush on her knuckles and fingers and under her nails, rubbing at her upturned palms with Laura peering into them—'All gone, Mummy?'—until she started to cry, 'No more dirty!', trying to get out of the water, slippery like a fish and no one could have caught her. It seemed as if something in her daughter, too, had changed, she told me. That awful expression, 'No more dirty'—and realising how Laura continued to be in touch with the girl, in the hours they spent at the nursery together … it made her shudder. Thank goodness, she told herself, the baby and Tim hadn't become similarly infected. Bobby was with her most of the time, he was still at that age, so she knew he was alright, and Tim's class was full of nice, proper British children … But it was indeed starting to feel like a 'disease'—her word—since she had realised, back in the autumn, that there were foreigners moving into their special part of the neighbourhood, coming into the nursery next door to Oak Street Preparatory 'if you please', as the mothers had taken to saying, as if those people expected their children to begin their education there along with their own sons and daughters whose names had been on the waiting list since birth. It was shocking, they all agreed. The way there were so many of them, suddenly, with their strong-smelling foods and chattery languages none of the 'home mums', as they started calling themselves, would ever understand. 'I'm beginning to feel as though I'm the one who's the outsider,' was something Caroline Williamson had said just before Christmas at the drop-off by the front gate. 'After all, I'm the person paying to be here, and speaking the language others don't seem to!' She'd laughed at that, she said, and she laughed again, loudly and for a long time, when she told me—though none of it, as it turned out, was funny.

The fact is, the people were there. They'd moved in and were growing in numbers, all come through a charity that had been set up in association with their own nursery, she'd found out, which was educating them—'for free, with our money' as Sam Crighton-Smith put it—along with providing housing in the big mansion block down by the children's park. 'How does that work, eh?' Sam had asked, point-blank, shortly after a group of home mums had been to see the head of the nursery, lovely Mrs Alexander, who they might have thought would be on their side. For how could non-English speakers come in and take up places that were supposed to be reserved? That was not what they were paying private school fees for, was it? 'I mean, you go private to be … well, private,' was the way she put it—because none of the mothers could believe that this was happening here, in their part of Clapham, the really good part, where one expected to be protected from … 'all that'. But Mrs Alexander had just talked to them about understanding and patience and the need to open one's doors with generosity and grace, and a month later, more of the foreigners had arrived, and by January, there were seven families, someone had said, in all—from Syria, Afghanistan … Wherever there'd been some war or revolution those kinds of people were always having, only now here they were in Clapham—and God knows how many children between them. Seven families! That's about seven times seven! the cry went up at the book group. And half the women pregnant again, you could make it out under their robes or whatever it was they wore as they stood in the street outside with their prams and buggies taking up so much space it could be difficult to park your car. 'Actually would you mind,' said Lara Veale, after they'd finished the last international bestseller set in Calcutta by a Commonwealth prize-winning author, 'if we just read some nice ordinary English novel next week? I kind of feel up to here with multiculturalism.'

I remember how she put her head back when she told me that and laughed another of her strange loud laughs, with her mouth wide open. I felt my heart skip a beat. 'Look at me,' she said afterwards, when she'd stopped and regained her composure, returning again to express herself in her usual, measured, thoughtful, way. 'I should be ashamed of myself … Except—you know what?' She looked down at her beautiful hands, one laid on top of the other in a gesture that was poised, considered. 'I don't care one bit.'

This was on one of my very early visits. I'd been trying to press her further on those friends of hers, her close neighbours with their book groups and cinema outings to *Fifty Shades of Grey* and the coffee mornings and yoga sessions designed to get back their pre-baby tummies … I wanted to know whether the sense of unease that was building—I meant, generally, among the mothers in the street and surrounding area—gave a sort of … context, I suppose, for the strength of her own reactions. The 'What has the country come to?' kinds of remarks that had started a while back, when she'd realised she was by no means the only one in our street to have voted Leave, gaining traction with the recent developments? But no. She always returned to the same version of her narrative; that it was all her. Her decision. Her plan. That she'd known for some time that something about her nature meant she needed, absolutely had to have, a specific sort of order to her days; to be in control, with everything in its place. That it really was only her idea, and that it was most definitely the foreign child and the smell of her, an odour she couldn't bear, now transferred to her own daughter, that was the 'trigger', as she put it, and made a little gesture with her two fingers, pointing them together at me as she mouthed the word 'ka-pow!'

That was it, as I record it: This woman. This neighbour. This friend. A simple case of 'cause and effect'—as she herself would put it—that eventually, unbelievably, played out on that late spring morning in April, which in turn had been set off earlier in the year when she picked up Laura at lunchtime as usual and Laura had asked if she might go home with the little girl she was holding hands with as she came out of the classroom, Tami, Laura said her name was, to

Pakistan for a playdate. 'Pakistan!' She couldn't believe what she was hearing. That her daughter even knew such a place existed, let alone wanted to spend time with a child who might have come from there. 'You can't go to Pakistan for a playdate,' she'd said, 'Don't be silly.' But Laura had held onto the child's hand, saying, 'Please! I want to go to Tami's! I want to!'—and yes, she told me, it was then, precisely, that she recognised how a kind of judgement she'd always held but that no doubt had been made worse by the changes taking place in the neighbourhood had collected around that moment, with her own daughter holding the filthy hand of some little scrap of a girl and not letting go, the mother standing there at the gate beside them in a greasy-looking black robe and the gold in her nose and all the rest of it, nodding and grinning, 'Okay? Okay?' like some kind of performing monkey. Her having to deal with that, she said, and having to say to Laura, 'Not today, sweetie,' and then again, louder, because Laura wasn't listening, the two little girls swinging their hands together and smiling at each other and talking their heads off and laughing. 'God,' she shook her head, when she first told me this part of the story, when she spoke about it for the first time. 'I relive it'—the feeling of all the pieces that she had put carefully in place in her life being smashed out of order, something happening that, to her mind, never, ever should have. It had taken 'ages', apparently, to get Laura finally to let go of the other girl and come with her, by which time there'd been tears and a massive row in front of everyone. She'd found herself short of breath as they got down the street, trying to put the situation behind her, because she'd had a sensation, 'just here,' she told me, touching her solar plexus, 'when Laura asked, you know, if she could go to this child's house, with the mother standing by and … there was this smell. Coming off the pair of them. Passed from the other girl straight onto Laura, I can't describe it. But I can tell you it made me feel sick.'

As I say, that was sometime around the middle of January, when she'd first registered the shift in herself as something physical, thoughts lying low but already sensible to her by then, insistent. There'd been her catch of breath, a lack of air, the tension in the upper part of her torso with the feeling of her daughter being drawn away from her, as though she was pulling away from her own mother, and then never getting the smell off her afterwards, was how it seemed, no matter how much she tried, scrubbing and scrubbing to try and get her clean, the way the child reacted to her when she came near at bath times, 'No, no, mummy, please!' backing away, 'No more dirty!' like a little animal.

And all this was still well before she'd even thought of taking the next step, figuring out that she was going to need two guns and so on, that there'd be no time to reload and that the guns would have to be small. I've been clear about that in my notes. 'You see, I realised I couldn't stop my daughter playing with the Pakistani girl,' was how she put it. That Laura continued to talk about her when she came home after nursery, 'Tami, this, Tami that …' And that though she no longer saw them together—such was the sure effect of her threat of punishment if she did—she knew the friendship was there, embedded. Out of sight, maybe, within the nursery grounds and walls, but alive and growing, and not only between Laura and the other, who had both started it, she knew, her own daughter the first to let it in, but festering by now among all the children, multiplying and getting stronger while they were playing together, sharing food and toys and glasses of juice …

These were the sort of ideas, you understand, that were present in her mind, and ran amok there. I'm simply reporting them, the circumstances surrounding this one woman who we all liked and got on with, who had lovely manners and was beautifully turned out and so on, and thoughtful, always helping out with bits of shopping or taking someone else's child for the morning while the mother was busy ... to put in all the details as though to come closer to the facts surrounding those most awful facts. For though by now the whole story is 'dead', as journalists would say, and as she has no other visitors, I have been allowed to meet with her, once a month in prison visiting hours, just to talk. It's something someone at our church first recommended, then our vicar got on board. 'Go in there,' John said to me when I was discussing the matter with him after one of the morning services—this, days after the thing had happened and everyone was in shock, the church open all night with prayer vigils and so on. 'You were someone who knew her,' he said. 'She needs to know that despite it, despite everything, the Church is open to her. That we, her congregation, despite the magnitude of her crime, still love her, can forgive.'

Not everyone can, though. Not her husband, he was the first to move away, with his mother having taken the other children to Hampshire, I heard. Not Pam Lawrence or Susan MacLeod or Jennifer Morris or the Caxton-Taylors or the Williamsons or any of the other families we know who were affected. Not a lot of people could consider it, even, or come close to understanding her by having any kind of sequence of events laid down on paper, the background to the fateful day, the outburst itself that left two children dead and seven injured, Catriona Morris without an eye, the little Williamson boy still in hospital and no one knowing if he'll ever come out. Though John was right, it is something we need to find out about, the whys and wherefores, and so, yes, I might not have been in the group she was close to—those women with their at-home Pilates lessons and pedicures and all the rest of it, their online porn and shopping sites and the husbands with big financial and legal jobs in the City—still, she and I had started chatting at St Cuthbert's when we used to teach Sunday School together ... so I need to remind people somehow that, you know, everyone around here always thought she was lovely.

And it was never Catriona Morris and the others that she meant to hurt—you might have guessed as much, of course. It was something, rather, that she only wanted to 'nip in the bud' for herself, she said, to do with the particular odour that was spreading and infecting—all these phrases of hers—as a result of circumstances that should never have been present at a three-and-a-half-thousand-pounds-a-term nursery in the first place. For anyone could see where it would all lead, she told me. The next thing, the same charity helping these same people get into the classrooms next door. Taking up the teaching allocation with special lessons for them to learn English—and then what would happen when it came time for the 11-plus for the British children, what then? And after that? With secondary schools and university? Oxford and Cambridge and all the rest of it? When it came to jobs and careers and security? What then? What then? Anything could happen ... anything ... was where her own thinking was headed, she told me. And truthfully? It had been taking her there for a very, very long time, with nobody around to talk to about it, not really, and Charles never there to listen or discuss any of it ... only away or working every hour God gives at Merrill Lynch along with all the other husbands in the street, working twice as hard as they should have to because of Austerity and China and the Asians coming in and getting the top finance jobs, and a lot of companies relocating back to the States or Europe after the no-deal mess London was in ... and it had been compounding and amassing, her way of thinking, building up for months beforehand, for months and months, years even ... until there appeared before her, out of the chaos, the little girl who wouldn't let go of Laura's hand and Laura herself—this the worst part of all, she said—not wanting to let go.

So alright, that's where we've got to, as I told John. Putting together so-called unrelated events, as they described it in the papers, and trying to make sense of how those seemingly disparate factors might pile up and end with the story of a woman who opened fire at her daughter's nursery while the children were outside on an Easter egg hunt, the two young women who were looking after them that day calling out 'warm!' and 'warmer!' as the children roamed around the flower beds and beneath the trunks of trees, looking for the foil-wrapped chocolates that had been placed there. 'Hot!' they may have shouted, as the first gunshot rang out. 'Scalding!' before they realised what had happened.

Because 'unrelated'—no. Nothing is without consequences or goes forward without the drive that lies behind. All of us know that. 'I just wanted to be able to breathe again,' was how she put it, how she described being in that linen cupboard of hers—the exact kind you see replicated all over those big double-fronted houses in South West London; 'leafy environs' is the wording on the estate agents' glossy brochures. A beautiful walk-in linen cupboard, as she has told me about many, many times, so generously proportioned there was even room in there for a little stool that her mother had embroidered the cushion for when Tim was born, in cross-stitch, with a flower border and *Where do we live but in the days?* worked in a panel in the centre. During some of her own days, she told me—this long before any of it, before the purchase of the guns, before the families came, before Bobby was born, even—she would go into the cupboard to sit on that little stool and close the door and stay there, quietly, on her own, for some time in the dark.

Just to have a sense, she said, of everything being gathered up, and clean and orderly in the same way that the laundry service would deliver clean nappies on a Monday and the neat stacks of all her children's clothing would be there on the third shelf, piled up every week in tidy rows, every week the same ... Was that such a big ask? To want everything to be as she'd planned it? A whole life arranged according to the values she'd always believed in, with nothing to expect but what she'd asked for, and all traces of unpleasantness, of any kind of difficulty, gone? She looked at me when she said that and smiled, but a sad smile this time, there was no laughter in it. 'Remember,' she said, and this right from the outset, when the whole project of assembling this story first began, with John and the church arranging my prison visits, my getting to know her more as she talked about everything that had gone on in that low voice of hers that is modulated and well-educated, and reasonable and low. 'I shot my own daughter first.'

Afterword:
Night-Scented Stock

Mary Masterson was never someone short for words, but when she got home after the book reading and saw the bouquet waiting at the front door, language left her. She simply stood there, aghast.

The flowers were enormous. Great fatted chrysanthemums held by skinny stems jostled up next to double-headed tulips and phlox; massed foliage poked out above the many greasy hearts of lilies. And were those thistles? Yes. Thistles, too, and other unkind-looking items were arranged among the rest. This was a posy with no theme or unity—and was it even … fresh? There was something about the dryness in some areas, a sponginess in others, that suggested otherwise, reminding Mary of the event she'd just attended, the launch of a collection of short stories that was called *Pretty Ugly*.

Despite her doubts, when she picked the bouquet up, enormous as a baby, the same Mary felt an emotion rise within her she couldn't have named. Not right then. Something to do with implacability. Wretchedness. But something, too, that spoke of generosity and love. Who had sent this item to her? What was it about the arrangement that so wanted to be brought inside and placed in a vase—or vases—that these blooms would be present all through her house?

She balanced the bundle on one hip while she jiggled for the front door key. The word tenderness came into it, for sure. A feeling of: *Don't worry. Give me just a minute.* Of: *Here we go. And be careful, be careful ...* As though past years, with all their clamours and cries, those thin young voices, had come back to her in echoes. *Mum? Are you there? Will it be ok?*

For the posy had indeed gone to dryness and to rot. One may as well admit it. And again, who would do such a thing? Send a gift in this condition? And there was no note. No card. Though here she was, Mary Masterson, carefully, tidily bringing the whole fragile, unwieldy package indoors and laying it down with complete and utter gentleness upon the table in the hall. As though part of her past self was caught up in that gesture, that mother, with that child. The words, *What are you?* being asked so quietly, hesitantly, so as not to disturb. *Do I know? Can I help?* While the base papers of the blooms' wrappings dripped. One, two. And the flowers' heads were peeping, sweetly, sweetly, from above the inner lining of the bouquet's tissue.

At the reading earlier it had seemed to Mary that speech, description, having the right words ... had been all. The characters in those stories, their talk, the author herself describing how the idea of *Pretty Ugly* had come about, her thinking around themes connected to society and ambition and capitalism and how much an individual life could bear ... There'd been plenty to upset Mary, she'd acknowledged that. There'd been much about the fiction she hadn't liked or wanted to admire, even. Still, at the same time, she had listened carefully to everything she'd heard. Her mind had been full—absolutely—of responses to the characters and their situations; her opinions, reactions, as though sections of her own prose rising up in her like a crowd of people she herself had invented.

But now? Here she was with this bouquet—at this point in her own story—and with little to say. Why accept it? That this gift might strip her language bare? Might leave her only carrying the thing, bearing it—for look, here it was back in her arms. This ... 'loveliness'. For she realised at that second that that was the word for it exactly. Loveliness, yes—and so why not then discover what it might mean for her, where it might lead?

Coming down the hall to stand in the centre of her bright kitchen, Mary felt the press of the flowers upon her. Early summer, the window open—and the few dishes in the sink quite rinsed and with nothing more to do, why would there be?—she could take her time with planning her next move. In the clarity of the evening light, she could see the variety of the bouquet, tiny near-dead freesias among the chrysanthemums and thorns, pale pinks and lavender coming up sharp and sweet. There was that memory again of the babies sleeping—amid the same blooms' pulp and decay. There must be something about all this, Mary thought. Something ... she could use. Her mind returned to the bookshop—and how nothing at that reading had seemed to fit. Those stories had been all over the place. There'd been the strangeness of the people, real but not real; the weirdly compacted mixture of their activities and emotions. It was a book, *Pretty Ugly*, that had been filled with incidents that just didn't add up. And yet. Mary drew breath. There had indeed been an element about it, like the flowers she had before her, that was fragrant and appealing, while also vegetal. Like a good stock perhaps? And cut the stems up very fine? Why not? Use the best of the petals for garnish later? Then invite some people round, maybe, and make of the entire bouquet a delicious soup?

There it lay—there on the bench. Its papers were still on and all in a piece, but here Mary was with this new and very very real idea taking shape in her mind—words, phrases forming and gathering in the way the same people in the collection of stories seemed to have made of something awful something else. Like that family living wild in the country or the woman who, despite awful confusion and concern, fell in love with a kitten come dancing out from under a pile of junk. Or that man in another story who'd seemed bloated to her, to Mary Masterson—a woman not normally short of words, remember—but whose wretched condition had also contained within it a great deal of tender and prolonged desire.

So alright, then—Mary thought. Go to it. She was ready. First rushing upstairs to check that the bedrooms were indeed empty— the children grown up and left, the family gone—then back down to the kitchen and into a drawer for the knife. Within seconds, she had an onion frying slowly in a pan and no need for herbs with everything that was happening beneath the florist's waxed paper. All it would take now, she was certain, was the fine, fine chopping to make a really good soup—rose, nasturtium, night-scented stocks—a recipe taking shape that may as well be a completed short story of her own. A thing that had been beautiful once, now wrecked, soon able to be eaten. Her children moving softly in their sleep upstairs as though they were still there and the whole house alight with sunshine and the stink of stock and nourishment and beauty and kindness. This … loveliness. Yes. This was.

Acknowledgements

Many thanks to the editors and publishers of the following publications, where some of the stories in this collection (or earlier versions) originally appeared:

'Blackjack' in *The New Zealand Listener* (January 2024); 'Dangerous Dog' in *Reader, I Married Him* edited by Tracy Chevalier (London: HarperCollins, 2016); 'Flight Path' in *Prospect* (December 2022); 'King Country' in *The Montréal Review* (July 2021); '"It is lonely being a young man sent abroad to fight," she said' in *Matraga* v. 27 n. 51 (2020); 'Mam's Tables' in *Newsroom* (August 2022); 'Poor Beasts' in *The Land Agent: 1700–1920* edited by Lowri Ann Rees, Ciarán Reilly and Annie Tindley (Edinburgh: Edinburgh University Press, 2018); 'All Gone' in *Landfall 244* (Spring 2022).

The author is also grateful for a Visiting Research Fellowship at Merton College, Oxford, where she worked on stories for this book, and to Sue Wootton and the team at Otago University Press for the scrupulous attention, care and enthusiasm with which they have brought this publication together. Thank you!

Published in New Zealand by Otago University Press
Te Whare Tā o Ōtakou Whakaihu Waka
533 Castle Street
Dunedin, New Zealand
university.press@otago.ac.nz
www.oup.nz

First published 2024
Copyright © Kirsty Gunn

The moral rights of the author have been asserted.

ISBN 978-1-99-004889-0

A catalogue record for this book is available from the National Library of
New Zealand. This book is copyright. Except for the purpose of fair review, no
part may be stored or transmitted in any form or by any means, electronic or
mechanical, including recording or storage in any information retrieval system,
without permission in writing from the publishers. No reproduction may be made,
whether by photocopying or by any other means, unless a licence has
been obtained from the publisher.

Editor: Mel Stevens
Design/layout: Fiona Moffat

Front cover: Ann Shelton, 2022, *We thank you for the gift to decide the fate of man
from birth (apple)*, archival pigment print on Hahnemühle Bamboo paper.

Printed in New Zealand by Ligare